FACE TO FACE
WITH AN ALIEN
ECO-THREAT

He was a rebuilt human being, with superhuman physical powers and a mind like a computer. His name was Subble and he was up against the intelligent *mantas*, a half-understood threat three explorers brought back from another world. And the explorers themselves were an enigma: two men and a woman, each with bizarre neurotic tendencies and an emotional involvement that was somehow symbolic of the alien menace itself.

Only a superman like Subble could disentangle the psychological and biological web and meet the aliens in a battle of minds and, ultimately, of life and death.

OMNIVORE

PIERS ANTHONY

AVON
PUBLISHERS OF BARD, CAMELOT AND DISCUS BOOKS

AVON BOOKS
A division of
The Hearst Corporation
959 Eighth Avenue
New York, New York 10019

First Avon Printing, October, 1978
Third Printing

AVON TRADEMARK REG. U.S. PAT. OFF. AND IN
OTHER COUNTRIES, MARCA REGISTRADA,
HECHO EN U.S.A.

Printed in U.S.A.

CONTENTS

OMNIVORE

1. A Loaf of Bread

NORTH OF APPALACHIA an outcropping of wilderness survived. Subble aligned visible topography with known coordinates and guided his craft to a soft landing beside a thickly-spoked bull spruce. The distinctive gum smell of it surrounded him as he stepped out, and decades of rotting needles crunched underfoot.

The measured ring of steel striking hardwood led him past a grossly twisted yellow birch and into a subforest of tall beech trees. The forest was rather pleasant, in a disordered way; it occurred to him that few places on Earth remained so close to Nature's original.

The sound that had seemed so near was actually some distance away. Subble threaded his way through a thicket of young ash and maple and came at last to a forest trail: two slick brown ruts cut in the leafy floor. Clusters of toadstools sprouted periodically along it, and he spied one large bracket fungus embracing a decaying stump. Tiny gnats found him and hovered tirelessly before his eyes.

The trail debouched into an artificial clearing formed by a felled beech. A man stood facing away from him, one booted foot braced against the scarred trunk, his broad back flexing as he swung a heavy axe. The lumberman was powerful; it showed in the checkered bulge of sleeve and in the smoothness of the swing. Chips scattered with every second connection as the blade bit a growing triangular section from the base of a hefty branch.

The limb severed and crashed into a leafy jungle beyond the trunk. The man turned and saw Subble, balancing the axe in his left hand while wiping the sweat off his forehead with a meaty right forearm. "Yeah?" he inquired, scowling.

This was the ticklish part. "I'm an investigator," Subble said, and kept his distance.

The man stiffened. Subble noted the slight elevation of the tendons along the back of the hand holding the axe, the sudden creases in a normally amiable face, and the slight shifting of weight. "Yeah?"

"All I want is information. If you are Vachel Smith, social code number 4409—"

"Cut it. I been Veg ten year and I ain't a number yet."

Subble ignored the tone and the exaggerated accent. "All right, Veg. I got a job, same as you, and I got to do it if I like it or not. Sooner we—"

Veg threw the axe at the beech stump, where it caught neatly, the handle vibrating. He closed his fists and took one step forward. "Last time a damn city slicker talked down to me, I broke his collarbone. Speak your piece and get out."

Subble smiled. "Very well—I'll stick to my own language. But I must have your cooperation. There is information nobody else can provide."

"Yeah? What?"

"I don't know. That's why I have to ask."

"You don't know!" Veg seemed uncertain whether to laugh or swear, and his accent eased considerably. "You come poking into my lot and you don't even know what you're looking for?"

It was best to keep him asking questions. "That's right."

But Veg did not keep asking. "Mister, you're trying to make a fool out of me." He moved in.

Subble blew his breath out audibly in a controlled show of exasperation. He was not as large as the lumberman nor as heavily muscled, but he did not back off. "If you attempt to force me off your premises by physical means, I will have to employ certain defensive techniques at my command," he said as Veg advanced.

"Yeah?" Veg leaped.

Subble stepped aside and put his right foot forward as Veg's right fist came at his head. He jammed his right toe against Veg's, bent his knees, grabbed the big man's shirt, spun around counterclockwise and threw him over his shoulder.

Veg landed in the slippery moist earth of the trail, unharmed and undismayed. "Yeah!" he said again, and launched himself a second time.

Subble ducked, caught Veg in the stomach with a shoulder block and followed it up with a quick and effective series of grips about the neck and shoulders.

Veg kept his feet, but his head lolled and both arms dangled. Subble let him catch his balance and recover the use of his extremities. "I gave you fair warning."

The lumberman shook himself and stretched his head from side to side. "Yeah," he said.

"Now I have to talk with you, because that's my job. I'll leave as soon as I have what I need. I'm willing to trade for what I get."

"Mister, nobody ever bought me yet."

"Nobody offered to. You take a break and I'll fill in for as long as it takes you to talk. That way you won't lose any time and I'll be out of your way in a hurry."

Veg laughed, his good humor seemingly restored by his setback. "You sure are a determined cuss. There aren't any fancy nerves you can pinch on a bolt of beech, mister. I don't know you and I won't tell you a thing."

Subble was careful not to threaten the man. He looked around at the divergent timber, spotting a shy cinnamon-brown thrush with indistinct spots on its breast. "Veery," he said.

Veg followed his gaze. "Yeah, I know him," he said more softly. "Comes around every two, three days. Got a hermit thrush, too—state bird, you should hear him sing! Never found the nest, though." Then he remembered whom he was talking to and scowled again.

"I must have been pretty clumsy to set you against me so quickly." It was a calculated overture.

"Mister, it's not you. Anyone who knows a veery when he sees one has some good in him. It's the government. We don't truck much with—you really don't know what you came for?"

"An agent's memory is washed blank before every assignment. I have been given three addresses and a caution signal. That was, literally, all I knew about

12

you before I landed. Your name, where to find you, and a warning of danger."

"That's crazy!"

"It prevents me from approaching the case with a bias. Everything must come from the case itself, nothing from my expectations or records which may be incomplete or distorted."

"But if you don't even know what—I mean, I could lie to you and you'd never guess. I could tell you I'm a petty thief on the lam—"

"You aren't."

"I thought you said you had no—"

Subble glanced at the tree again, but the bird was gone. So, oddly, were most of the other ubiquitous creatures of the forest. Something had subdued them. "I was given no information, but my training enables me to obtain it very quickly. I know a good deal about you now."

"Okay, Mister what's-your-name—"

"Subble."

"Mister Government Agent. *How* do you know I'm not a thief?"

"I can give you a general idea. I'm equipped to pick up your respiration, heartbeat, muscle tension, the nuances of facial expression, vocal inflection, subvocal—"

"You saying you can tell when I'm lying just by watching me?"

"Yes. You are not a devious man."

"I'm not a liar, either. But I'm not so sure about you."

Subble took no offense. "You are wise. I *am* a devious man. I am fully capable of lying when my mission requires it, and I am an expert at it."

Veg touched his sore neck. "More than that, I guess."

"Yes—I could have maimed you or killed you. But that's my specialty, and I don't misuse my training any more than you would misuse your axe, or destroy that thrush's nest. You *could* cut down every sapling in the forest—"

"God, no! This's fourth generation timber now. I'm just cleaning out the weed trees and—" He paused. "Yeah, I guess I see what you mean. You don't go 'round hurting people for the fun of it. But you still can't find out a thing if I don't talk to you."

"I'm afraid I can, if there is no alternative."

Veg studied him with genuine curiosity. "How?"

"By making statements, asking questions, and reading your reactions."

"Okay. I'm going to shut up now. You tell me what you learn."

"You may not like this, Veg."

The man picked up his axe and returned to the trunk he had been limbing.

"Are you a vegetarian?" Subble asked. "Yes, you are," he answered himself immediately.

"You already knew!" Veg shouted, shaken. "You wouldn't even've *asked* that question if you didn't know!"

"I knew—but you were the one who told me. Your nickname, for one thing, and the smell of your breath, and your tension when I mentioned killing. You haven't touched meat for a decade."

Veg's mouth was tight. "Tell me something you couldn't've found in a government snoop-file," he said. He didn't bother to chop any more.

"If you will put down your weapon—"

"Weapon? Oh." He pitched the axe at the stump, missing this time.

"You see, you're upset now—and I would have to act precipitously if you were to attack me with *that*. Are you sure you—"

"Go ahead. Prove it."

Subble's voice was low, but he watched Veg very carefully. "Are you interested in baseball? ... No. Shakespeare? ... No. Any other playwright? ... Yes. Modern? ... Yes, but not *too* modern ... American? Foreign? ... Ah, English? Shaw, of course!"

Veg started to say something, but didn't. Stronger medicine was required before he would be convinced.

"How about women? ... Yes and no. Not just *any* woman. Are you in love? ... Yes, I see that you are, and not casually, but there is something wrong. Is she pretty? ... Yes, lovely. Have you slept with her, man to woman? ... No? But you aren't impotent ... No! Would she let you? ... She would, probably. Her name is Aquilon—"

Veg's lunge missed by several inches. "Easy! The name happens to be the second on my list," Subble explained. "It was logical, in the circumstance, that she would be the one you—now don't charge me again."

The big man halted. "Yeah, you did warn me. Again." He looked at Subble with a certain difficult respect. "I guess I believe you."

"I don't want to pry into your private affairs. All I want is the information I was sent for. My offer stands. If you want anything for your trouble—"

"Mister—Subble, you said?—you have more on

the ball than I figured. But I already said: it's not you. It's the government. That's trouble every time. I have a notion what you came for, and I can't tell you. Not when some bureaucrat's going to—"

"I'm not an ordinary agent. What you tell me is held in confidence. I gather the information, assimilate it and make a single verbal report from which all irrelevancies are excluded. I may need to learn some personal matters in order to pursue my investigation and draw conclusions, but no one else need know."

"You sound pretty sure of that."

"I am sure. I'm sorry my word is worthless, since I could and would easily break it. I'll just have to assure you unofficially that I could be lying now, but am not. Your relationship with Aquilon has no relevance to—oh, oh."

"Yeah. Just me and you, okay. But it isn't. It's my friends and the government, and I just don't have the right."

Subble had expected something like this. The nature of the assignment was beginning to take shape, and he was now in a position to obtain a great deal from Veg—but his very training in prevarication, as with that in combat, made him exceedingly careful of the rights of others. An agent who gained his ends ruthlessly was apt to be unsuccessful in the end, since force inevitably inspired counterforce. And it was not wise to act in a manner that would increase the general distrust of agents as a whole. There was danger—extreme danger, he suspected now—and not from Veg himself. It was essential that no personal antagonism be added to it.

"Veg, I have all day, as far as I know, and

tomorrow too. I'm not on a schedule, but I do have to get at the facts, whatever they may be. How about letting me stay with you for a few hours, so we can get to know each other, and you can tell me as much as you feel free to. I won't push you for any more than that, once you draw the line, and you'll have the confidence that you are not simply spouting off to a stranger."

"What if I decide to tell you nothing?"

"Then you tell me nothing."

Veg thought about it, scratching his sandy head. "You going to talk to 'Quilon?"

"I have to. And Calvin. And anybody else who knows—whatever it is."

"And you don't report till the end, just a summary?"

"That's right."

"I guess I'd better, then. God, I sure don't like it, though."

Subble smiled, but not inside. He could see that Veg had grave misgivings, and not on purely personal grounds. There *was* danger, and Veg knew it, and it was personal and immediate.

"I understand that you do not bear me any more than residual ill-will," Subble observed. "You respect physical ability, as many strong men do. But you are afraid that if I learn too much, I will be harmed or killed, and that will make real trouble. I mention this only so that you will be aware that I know. And you are right: while I do not fear death, if I do die there will be a thorough and official investigation. You know what that means."

"Yeah," Veg said unhappily.

Subble dropped the subject. It was always difficult

to obtain the trust of a normal person, but always necessary. He believed that frankness was best, and before long it would occur to Veg that he would be well advised to see that the agent got enough information at least to preserve his life. "How can I help?"

"Well—" Veg looked about, searching for some pretext to accept the inevitable. "Say—there *is* a little matter I've been saving up for a special occasion. This way."

He trotted down the fresh logging track, intersecting another trail and following that. Subble saw the prints and ordure of horses, animals rarely seen today but still used in these protected tracts. Machines of all types were banned here; men harvested trees with hand tools and hauled out the logs with animal labor. Anyone who didn't care for the physical life was invited out in a hurry. There were too many people and too many machines in the world, and the fringe wilderness was a jealously guarded area.

Veg angled away from the trail, brushing by the round leaves of a young basswood and the serrated ones of the maples to jump over an ancient stone wall. Over a century ago men had built such walls by hand, using the great chunks of rock they cleared from their fields; such a wall had inspired the poet Robert Frost to discourse upon its mending, but no one cared to mend it now.

A sitting chipmunk dropped its acorn and scurried silently away. "Sorry, pal—didn't see you," Veg muttered as the handsome striped body disappeared. He pulled up under a huge blazed beech and put his hands to his mouth. "Yo, Jones!" he yelled.

In a few minutes two dark men appeared and

came to stand beyond the tree. "What'sa matter—lonesome?" one inquired with blunt sarcasm. He was a husky individual, smaller than Veg but sure of himself. He wore the standard denims and checkered shirt, and a small neat mustache. His companion was similar, lacking the mustache.

"Naw," Veg said. He put his hands on his hips aggressively. "Remember that business about this boundary last month?"

"You mean when you tried to poach on our territory?"

"I mean when you hauled the marker-stone twenty feet out of line and claimed three of my best white ash and a rock maple." He gestured, and Subble saw the stone some distance beyond.

"*Re*claimed, you mean."

"And I said I'd take care of it when the time came."

The two men nodded, smirking.

"Well, the time's come," Veg said.

The mustached man approached. "That your second?" he asked, glancing disparagingly at Subble. "A city slick?"

"That's my second. Name's Subble." He turned to Subble. "This is Hank Jones. He and his brother work this lot next to mine—and some of mine, too."

"City duds!" Jones said. "Well, I reckon bound'ry jumpers can't be choosy." He unlimbered a roundhouse left at Veg.

It was grandiose and clumsy by Subble's standards, but basic rules were evident. The two men moved out into the clearing beyond the tree, exchanging ferocious blows and taking almost no evasive action, but the object seemed to be to beat the

19

opponent into submission without doing irreparable damage. Fists, feet and heads were freely employed, but never fingers or teeth, and eyes and crotches were left alone. Jones' brother called lewd encouragement and advice to his side, but did not interfere.

Veg took the first blow on the ear and shrugged it off. His own fist drove into Jones' belly, forcing the man away. Jones charged back headfirst, butting with such power that Veg fell to the ground. As he rolled to hands and knees, Jones put his boot up and shoved him down again, following this with a hard kick with the side of the boot to the shoulder. Toe-points also outlawed, Subble surmised, and heel-stomping.

Veg growled and leaped, fists alternating like pistons even before they met the target. He backed Jones against the beech and blasted mercilessly at his midsection until the man doubled over.

Jones' brother edged toward the pair, and Subble also moved in. Veg was an independent sort, and would not have accepted a "second" unless he deemed it necessary.

The combatants bounced away from the tree, dirty and sweaty but with undiminished energies. Veg backed off to recover his balance, and Jones' brother surreptitiously poked a stick between his feet. Veg tripped, and Jones was on him immediately.

Subble strode across the arena and stood before his opposite number. "Friend, if you want to participate, pick your own fight," he suggested.

The man scowled and swung. The attack was incredibly crude—but Subble accepted the blow on the shoulder and replied with a moderate jab to the gut. He had no need of his special skills here, and preferred not to display them. Obviously these encounters were family affairs, and all interested parties participated.

The single fight had become two—and privacy had dissipated. Only partially concerned with the mock-fight he was engaged in, Subble watched and listened to the other lumbermen as they emerged from the forest on all sides, until a great circle of cheerful faces surrounded them.

The sounds of extracurricular activity penetrated a long distance, it seemed, and the neighbors wasted no time dealing themselves in.

"Veg and Hank Jones are settling their account, as I make it," one man explained to his companion. "My guess is the stranger was standing in for Veg's second, and figured to keep Job Jones out of it. City man."

"I'll second the stranger," the other said. "He's holding up his end okay, considering."

"Yeah?" a third put in. "I'm for Job."

"Son, you picked a loser. Neither Jones can last long without his brother."

The third raised his fist. "*I'm* his brother, far as you're concerned."

And the third fight commenced. In like manner the two new antagonists were seconded, and soon a fourth battle was underway.

Subble laughed inwardly. He had been right: fighting was as much pleasure as business to these hardy folk, and any pretext would do. They could not stand idly by and let others war; they had to join in. But it was man to man, not group to group.

He ducked a swing from Job Jones and butted him in approved fashion. Job backed into another contestant, jarring the other man's aim as he cocked his fist. "Sorry," Job muttered. "Forget it," the other said, and proceeded with his own concern.

The ring was crowded now, resembling a ballroom filled with strenuous dancers. It was impossible to tell for which side any given man stood—yet each pair remained distinct and no one intentionally struck anyone except his assigned antagonist. As in the dance, each couple created its discrete formations in the midst of babel. There even seemed to be music.

A hand fell upon his shoulder. "Your turn's up," Veg said jovially. "Take a seat."

Surprised, Subble broke. Job Jones quit immediately and went to the far side to join his brother, while Veg squatted down to view the melee. Hank Jones was playing a harmonica with some rude skill . . . so there *was* music now!

Before long the man who had seconded Subble joined them, his match lining up with the seated Joneses. New matches were still being formed from the uncommitted pool, distinguished by cleaner clothing and absence of bruises, and this in turn was constantly reinforced by arriving spectators. The men bore a common stamp of sturdy self-assurance and lusty living that contrasted with what Subble knew the city-norm to be.

"No room for everyone at once," Veg explained.

Someone hauled out a guitar and began strumming more or less in time with the harmonica, and another man took a stick and began setting the beat on the scarred beech.

Subble was astonished at the scope of the battle. A dozen pairs were brawling in the clearing, and as many more men were scattered about the fringe. Someone had hauled in a wagon bearing a monstrous keg of beer, and wooden mugs of the frothing liquid were being circulated along with pails of forest berries and triangular beechnuts.

Subble accepted a warm beer and took a swallow. The activity had made him pleasantly thirsty—that, he realized, was part of the point of all this. It was technically a malt beverage—but home-brewed to about twenty proof. He smiled; he was sure the local soft-liquor taxmen had never met this keg.

Veg noticed his reaction. "You didn't come for this?" he asked with sudden concern.

Subble drained his high-potency mug. "You know it ain't!"

This time Veg did not take exception to the language.

The battle waned as the beer fumes drifted. The active participants became ten, then eight, as each contest fissioned into thirsty individuals. The lines of the seated extended almost entirely around the circle, the men conversing contentedly and waving their mugs.

The show dwindled to two, and finally to a single encounter. The audience watched avidly now, rooting not so much for one man or the other as for the fight itself.

"Which one is ours?" Subble inquired, having lost track. "Or does it matter anymore?"

"It matters," Veg said. "I hope it's Buff. He's a good man."

Buff *was* a good man, and in due course he was conceded the victory. The last two grabbed mugs and gulped them pantingly as they plumped to the ground. The music finished with a flourish and an expectant silence came.

"Now the fun begins," Veg muttered. Then, loudly: "This meeting's to settle my boundary dispute with the Jones boys. Who did you second, Buff, you lop-eared bastard?"

"Not you, turnip!" Buff called back. He finished his beer. "I follow Zebra."

"You with me, animal?" Hank Jones yelled next.

"Naw, brushface," Zebra said. "I'm with Kenson."

And so it went, Veg and Jones taking turns challenging each ascending member of the victory chain, exchanging good-natured insults at every step while the keg gurgled to its steaming dregs and beechnut shells littered the ground. Long before the line finished Subble recognized its outcome, but refrained from comment.

"I follow this Fancy-Dan stranger here!" Subble's second proclaimed, and belched.

"And who the hell's *your* better man, you city refugee?" Veg shouted for the benefit of those who had joined the party too late to know.

"*You* are—in the daytime!" Subble cried. There was a burst of applause for the winner.

In moments a strong-backed crew had moved the boundary rock to the position Veg indicated, and an impromptu *a capella* group sang several verses of *The Frozen Logger*.

> I see that you are a logger,
> And not just a common bum—
> 'Cause nobody but a logger
> Stirs his coffee with his thumb!

Jones, it appeared, didn't feel like playing his instrument any more, but he did come up to shake hands. "I wasn't going to cut those trees," he said.

The crowd dissipated, the men returning to their separate plots, happy for the break. The beermaster hitched his team and tilted down the track. Subble wondered who paid the cost of such refreshment, and decided that there were probably standing arrangements. Perhaps, instead of logging, he brewed —but received an allotment from the lumber mill anyway. Whatever it was, the system seemed to be functioning smoothly.

Subble mouthed the conventionalities, but abruptly his attention was elsewhere. At the fringe of it all something deadly watched, hardly more than a dark shadow lost behind the trees. He focused his trained perceptions and picked up a momentary flicker, a suggestion of motion, a subdued whistle. As a wolf might glare at the fires of early man, waiting for the embers to die, waiting for sleep. . . .

"You did okay," Veg said, and the shadow was gone. Subble sniffed, but picked up only the rotting leaves and pushing fungus of the forest floor. He had lost it.

They tramped back to the original work area, the forest as empty as before, though Subble knew that many men were still within a mile. Soon the distant sounds of their labors would resume.

Veg's tongue had been loosened by several mugs of brew. "You catch on quick, and you fight fair once you get going. What do you make of our bunch?"

"It's a good bunch. I wish it were possible to—"

"Sub, don't start pulling that government-agent

reserve on me again. We've been through a party together, and we won!" But it was Veg's own reserve that had dissipated.

A party: fists and drink and a symbol of friendship. Why was it that men so often could only respect each other after testing their respective mettles in combat? Here it was physical; but in the more sophisticated, less open gatherings, male and female, it also went on continually. Men and animals measured each other before giving of each other, establishing, if not a pecking order, at least a nuance order. Was this a fundamental characteristic of life?

Subble regretted that he was not free to explore this thesis thoroughly. Agents were doers rather than thinkers, however their inclinations might run. "Well, there's little I can relate to," he told Veg. "My background is not like yours. I've never been to a—party—like this before. I was raised more conventionally."

Veg unpacked a collapsible saw from a cache in a tree. "I'm not exactly bright, but I know your education was not conventional," he said. He led the way to a pile of peeled spruce logs. "Grab an end and we'll get to know each other."

Subble accepted the proffered handle and fell into the rhythm of sawing. He knew that it was a matter of pull, not push, and that no weight should be applied; the saw's own weight would take it through the wood in its own fashion. The teeth were sharp and angled out alternately so that the cut was wider than the thickness of the saw; sharpening would be a tedious chore, but the saw worked well enough here.

What he hadn't known was the importance of a balanced, comfortable position that provided circulation for the legs and free play for arms and upper body. He was doing it incorrectly, and though he was not tired he knew that an ordinary man would wear out quickly this way.

Veg had marked off four foot lengths, and each time one bolt was severed he brought the next mark over the balancing point and began again. "Now take me," he said, pulling his end without noticeable exertion. "Folks take me for an ordinary, no-count joker who won't eat meat, and that's okay. But I have things I—"

He paused, and Subble knew that he had almost let slip something about the menace that had cast its strange eye upon the party. He certainly knew about it, and the matter was definitely relevant to Subble's mission; the signals were strong. But Veg was not yet ready to speak of this.

They sawed for a while. Subble copied Veg's stance, and finally caught on to the swing of it. The motions were relaxing, vaguely similar to the steady beat of waves upon a lonely shore, leading the mind to introspection. Jets of sweet-smelling sawdust splattered across his foot and into the top of his sock, giving him another lesson in woodsman's clothing. The curlicues settled on his toe were twisted lengths, some like little worms, rather than the powder he had expected. The texture would depend upon the nature and hardness of the wood, he thought.

"Well, like why I don't eat meat," Veg was saying instead of whatever he had intended. "It's okay to talk about how the world's too crowded, not enough places to live, not enough food to go around, everybody going crazy because there's no room to holler in. So they tell me I get a neurosis from all that, and

27

that's why I have to make it harder for myself. You believe that?"

"No," Subble said, sensing the proper answer to the ambiguous question. Veg was trying to come to grips with the problems posed by the frustration of the territorial imperative, though he evidently was not familiar with the terms. Every creature sought out a territory of its own, distinct from that of other representatives of its species; birds sang, in part, to define by sound the limits of their domains, their foraging grounds, and men liked to talk of their homes as being their castles. The contest he had just participated in had been a rather tangible manifestation of that need; it was important for Veg to know exactly where his boundaries were, even though the land was his only to the extent of limited cutting rights. Successful defense of those boundaries gave him a fundamental satisfaction; he had fought for his territory and won. Neurotic? Hardly; it was a return to normalcy.

"You're damn right, no. Those headshrinkers never set their twinkletoes in the forest. They've never been off-world. That's why—"

Once more that pause. Veg kept approaching the key and shying away.

"You're a vegetarian—and this is part of what I may have been sent to investigate," Subble said, helping him. "But you don't feel free to tell me just what the connection is."

"Yeah." They sawed for another period in silence. An inchworm mounted Subble's shoe, struggling to navigate the unsteady sawdust strings and freezing when it thought it was observed. All creatures had their problems and their frights, he thought. An inchworm hid itself in stillness; a man in silence.

Veg tried again. "Tell me if you ever heard anything like this. Maybe it makes sense to you. When I was a kid, my brother—well, he was a good guy. Everybody liked him. I liked him. We fought sometimes, but no real trouble—I mean, I had the muscle and he had the savvy, so we didn't feel crowded. We'd go around together all the time, but I knew he was the one going to make good. In the long run, you know, because of his brains. I didn't mind. He was right for it.

"Then he took sick. He was in the hospital, but he looked okay. I saw him there, and he said he felt fine, and that they told him he was going to be back in school again soon and to keep up with his studies. I guess that's the only time I was jealous of him, a little, 'cause all he had to do was lie around all day, while I had all those dull classes.

"Then he died. A teacher just came up and told me one day, that he'd gone the way they always knew he would. From the first day, almost, they'd known. Only they never told him that, or his friends, or me. Cancer—and all those doctors lying about it, telling us he was getting better and all, when he was dying. Them and their hypocritic oath. I didn't believe it at first; I used to dream he was still there, only he'd broken his leg or something and they thought it was real bad, but it got better after all, you know? I guess it took me a couple of years to believe he was gone, all the way down in my mind.

"And it got to me. I mean, here was my brother, a good guy, nobody had anything against him, but he died. And it got in my head, if there'd been this god—I don't believe in God—this guy looking down, saying 'One of these two boys has to go, there isn't room anymore for both,' and he had to make the choice, see . . . well, *I* was the one he should have taken, because I didn't have much to give the world anyway. You have to save the sheep and cast out the goat, or whatever, and he was the sheep.

"But this god took the wrong one. And there was this destiny, this good life, meant for my brother— and the wrong boy left to fill it. I was living *his* life, and it was all wrong, all wrong. But then I thought, now this mistake's been made, and it's too late to fix it, but it isn't all gone quite if I save as much as I can. What I have to do is, is—well, make something out of it the way he was supposed to make it, you know? Prove that maybe it wasn't a big mistake, just a small one, and not so much was changed after all."

They sawed another bolt in silence. The inchworm had negotiated the shoe and disappeared into the crushed leafery beyond, and the sawdust was mounding tremendously—three or four inches high. A swift fly had settled upon it, savoring its freshness, perhaps. The scene darkened alarmingly, then brightened as an unseen cloud crossed the sun. It was amazing how absorbing the microcosm became with a little concentration.

"Any of that make sense to you?" Veg inquired after a bit.

"Too much," Subble said, suffering a personal pang that surprised him.

"But it still hurt, knowing how he died," Veg said, encouraged. How often people were afraid to express their true feelings, for fear of ridicule, and so presented artificial ones instead. Veg was concerned because he had let slip the mask and failed to be artificial, but now it was all right. "I thought about it, and if there was one thing I was sure of, it was that death like that was wrong. I don't care what they say about statistics and survival—so many boys might've died, and him being the one that—but then I saw that those other boys were all somebody's brother too, you know, and probably if I knew them I'd know why they should live too. It wasn't all right to kill *anybody's* brother. And then I thought, what about the animals. . . .

"And when I stopped thinking, I wasn't killing anything that moved, or letting anybody else do it for me. It's as though that meat is *his* flesh."

"But you will fight," Subble observed.

"Yeah. I never did understand those pacifist types that preach nonviolence and demonstrate against war and then go home to a big juicy steak dinner. At least a man can fight *back*. Smack on the jaw doesn't hurt him, but—"

Subble moved so quickly that Veg, who was looking right at him, spoke the last several words and finished his stroke before realizing he was alone.

"Wha—?" But Subble was already coming back to resume sawing, disappointed. The menace at the fringe had moved faster yet, which deepened the mystery. Few animate things on Earth could elude an agent on the move.

"What kind of man *are* you?" Veg demanded somewhat belligerently. "You were just a blur—"

"I was after that thing. It's been stalking us all afternoon. I'm pretty sure that's what I was sent for."

"You *saw* it?" Veg made no pretense of ignorance, though this would have made little difference to Subble in any event.

"Only a flicker. Just enough to tell me it is animal and alien. You're fooling with strong medicine, Veg."

"Yeah." The big man seemed almost relieved to be committed. "But it isn't what you think. I don't know *what* you think, but it isn't that."

"I don't have an opinion. I was sent to gather information on a matter relevant to Earth security. I make no judgment and no final decision. When I tell you that thing is dangerous, that's observation, not opinion. It reacted faster than I did."

Veg's brow wrinkled. "Just because it got the jump on you, it's a threat to the world?"

"I'm a very quick man, Veg. My powers *are* a threat to any normal community, unless completely under control."

Veg was hostile again. "So why should I trust you at all?"

"It's not a question of trust. You have to take me for what I am and make your decisions accordingly."

"Okay—*tell* me what you are."

"I'm a special breed of government agent. I'll have to give you some background—"

"Give."

"This continent is lightly populated compared to some, but its economic and political organizations are still immensely complicated. Every facet contributes exponentially to the overall—" Subble saw that Veg wasn't following, so shifted his ground. "Take crime. If a woodsman murders his neighbor to get his cutting rights, the other lumbermen will have a pretty good idea who did it, won't they?"

"Yeah. Not too many secrets hereabouts."

"That's the 'isolated community' approach. Everybody knows everybody, and trouble is easily handled by the group. But suppose *I* killed someone here, and went back home in my flyer before anything was done about it?"

"Guess we'd have to report it to the sheriff. But it'd be pretty hard for him to—"

"Precisely. Crime is no longer simple when there are many communities involved and interacting, and so many conflicting interests. Your sheriff's estimate of the situation would be valueless in running me down, because he wouldn't *know* me or my motives. I could walk into any body shop in Appalachia and have my facial features modified, hair restyled and recolored, body profile altered by braces and injections—I could be quite unrecognizable to you in half an hour. Even if the sheriff had my exact identity— which he probably wouldn't—it could take enough time to run me down so that my lawyer could cover the evidence against me. And believe me, the changes a body shop could make in my physical appearance are as nothing compared to what a lawyer can do to my *legal* appearance."

"You telling me you can get away with murder?"

"Yes. In today's complex world, almost anybody can—if he knows how. All he has to do is avoid detection or capture for the few hours necessary to cover his traces—his legal ones—and the job of bringing him to justice becomes so complicated and expensive that it isn't worth making the attempt."

Veg shook his head. "I'm just a simple country boy. I'll take your word it's rough in the big city. What has that got to do with why you're here?"

"Obviously we can't let the murderers go free—or any other criminals. And that's only one section of the problem. What we need is a carefully trained and disciplined force of investigators who can wrap up most cases so quickly that complications never develop. Men who can be assigned at a moment's notice and take hold immediately. Men who have the brains and muscle to act on their own, but the discipline to be inhumanly fair. Men whose reports will be so similar that a central computer can correlate them without having to make adjustments for individual ignorance or bias."

Veg frowned again. "You still aren't answering my question."

Subble smiled in reply. "I'm almost there. You wouldn't let Jones' brother arbitrate your dispute with Jones, would you?"

"Hell no! He'd—"

"So you understand what I mean by bias. The trouble is every person on this world is biased in some manner, even if he doesn't want to be. But when thousands of reports are being submitted by thousands of agents on thousands of unique situations every hour, bias is a luxury we can't afford. The computer has to be sure that the case is accurately presented, or the report is worthless. Yet it can't send out a bunch of identical robots—"

"You *are* a man?" Veg demanded.

"I am a man—but not an ordinary one. That is, not ordinary in the usual sense."

"Cut the pussyfooting and *tell* me!"

"I'm a stripped-down human chassis rebuilt to computer-specifications—physical and mental."

"An android!"

"No. I am a man, with a man's memories and feelings. I was born and raised as you were, and I'm sure I had my problems and my successes—but the past I have *now* has been grafted on with the body."

Veg struggled with the concept. "You mean you aren't real? You can't—"

"I'm real—but not as I was born. Whatever I was was cut away, and the entire framework of the ideal agent substituted. My memories—all of them—are his memories, and my abilities are his abilities. There are thousands like me, male and female."

"Just so your report will be like someone else's?"

"More or less. It's not merely a matter of standardization, but conformity to the highest qualifications. I can do things that my original personality could never have achieved."

"Like moving in a blur," Veg agreed. Then, after a moment: "I guess I see why you understood about my filling in for my brother's life. That's what you're doing. You're another peavey made out of a cant hook—only you don't even *know* what you started out to be."

Subble decided not to inquire what the difference was between a peavey and a cant hook.

They had finished the sawing. Veg stood up and stretched cramped legs. "Sub, I guess I know everything about you I want to. I'll tell you as much as I can, but I can't tell you everything. I mean, I know more, but—"

"But there is Aquilon. I understand."

"Yeah. 'Quilon and Cal and the rest of it. And when I stop, you don't ask any more questions, you just get out of here and I won't see you again, okay?

And you don't poke around after what's in the forest, either."

"Agreed," Subble said. The discomfort normal people felt around the retread was a fact of his life, and did not disturb him. Perhaps some of the antipathy stemmed from the fact that agents only questioned people who had something to conceal. Veg had agreed to cooperate to a certain extent, and that was all that was required.

As Veg talked, Subble forgot the man's lingering homespun mannerisms and language and absorbed the episode as though it were his own. He imagined himself on a distant colony-planet, gazing at scenery unlike any on Earth, breathing through a filter in his nose and riding beside a lovely but unsmiling woman. . . .

* * *

"Don't smile, 'Quilon," the big man said, forearms flexing on the controls.

The girl beside him put both hands to her lips in a naturally graceful reaction, searching, as though afraid her features had betrayed her.

" 'Quilon," Veg continued, "you know you're a mir'cle of beauty in summer shorts. Be a shame to ruin it with a little smile, now."

Aquilon leaned over, unsmiling, to rest her forehead against his muscular shoulder. "Don't," she pleaded quietly.

Veg stared ahead, realizing that he had hurt her but not understanding why. The truth was that he rather admired Aquilon's composure; it lent her features a classic splendor that few living women possessed. He had known many smiling females and respected none; they were always to be found hanging around the spaceport, eager for his money and his muscle and most of all for his notoriety: a spaceman. The mature ones were competent—and expensive—and not always trustworthy. The teeners were agog with puppylike willingness, anxious to question him on what simply *had* to be exciting, and too often taking the more prosaic truth for some veiled criticism of their feminine worth.

He was not a philosophic man, apart from one area that he kept to himself, and craved little more than physical pleasure and honest companionship; but circumstances had forced cynicism upon him. He was unsatisfied, and when driven to probe the reasons for this had realized that it was because he was in fact a non-person. The dedicated women of the spaceport were eager for news of space and for proximity to it—though not eager to undertake off-world voyages themselves. They had little interest in the personal needs or feelings of the man within the uniform. They paid off in sex and thought that was enough. It was true that he needed sex—but that was only the physical side of the coin. Sex was minutes; what about the hours remaining?

Aquilon was different. First, she had come to space herself, and that was a definite signal of determination, talent and courage. Second, she was young and astonishingly beautiful—an almost foolproof formula for serious trouble in space. She gave no shred of encouragement to any man—but she needed a man, if only to protect her boundaries from other males.

She had come to Cal.

If the choice seemed ludicrous, it was quickly

apparent that it was not. Cal had no designs on her, and was knowledgable about many things. She could talk to him without affectation or defensiveness, and touch him without being forcibly reminded that they were male and female. She could sleep in his cabin safely, for he forced himself on no person in any way. Indeed, she served him by bringing him books from the ship's library, by making up his bunk and cleaning his instruments and buttoning his uniform for him the few times uniforms were used in space. Cal was not always strong enough to do these things for himself.

But no cne interfered. At first there had been little restlessness, but Veg had talked to the men in question and it passed.

"As with Ferrovius and the Roman courtier," Cal had remarked sagely. Veg had failed to comprehend, and so the little man explained. "Ferrovius was a character in Shaw's play *Androcles and the Lion*. He was constructed somewhat like you, Veg, and I think there would be a fair comparison in temperament too. He was an early Christian, back in the days when such faith was unfashionable, and pledged to nonviolence. When the Roman struck him on the cheek, he dutifully turned the other cheek—but then he suggested that the Roman should try a similar exercise. 'I sat up all night with that youth wrestling for his soul;' he tells us, 'and in the morning not only was he a Christian, but his hair was as white as snow.' "

After that Veg, who had little interest in literature, had taken the trouble to read the complete play, and had discovered that the Irish playwright himself was a vegetarian. Small cosmos.

At any rate, Veg had impressed upon the remaining complement of the ship that Cal was his friend. When Aquilon entered the picture, she became Cal's second friend. It was that simple. What upset her, upset Cal—and that in turn made Veg restless and brought about Ferrovian exercises of pacifism.

The relationship between Veg and Aquilon was somewhat cooler. It was absolutely polite, and there was even innocent banter, as there had been just now—but they did not quite understand each other, as the recent dialogue had just reminded him.

She touched his tense bicep. "I'm sorry, Veg. My fault."

"Naw," he said, grinning. Suddenly his world was bright, though what he viewed was not. He swung the tractor around one of the giant fungi, wrinkling his nose at the fetid odor he fancied he smelled. He squinted through the front screen, trying to penetrate the haze that covered the planet of Nacre. The level plain ahead became lost in the gloom, its foreground broken only by the massive fungoid growths ballooning out of the fertile dust.

"Are we near the mountains?" Aquilon asked, slender fingers toying with a small but rather special art brush. Veg grunted.

The tractor accelerated, forging through the thick atmosphere. The wind whipped into the open cockpit, carrying Aquilon's hair out in short blonde streamers. She faced ahead, inhaling deeply through the concealed nostril filters. She did not smile.

Veg eased up as the mountain ridge appeared. Nacre had never been mapped, largely because there was no economical way to do it, but men were working on the problem now, and he enjoyed exploring. The outcroppings at the base of these hills of his were stark, while the tops projected into the encompassing mist and vanished. Aquilon's fingers moved in air, shaping the vision she saw, eager to express it on canvasite.

"Look at the vegetation!" she exclaimed. "The toadstools!"

Now that they were moving slowly, Veg could see what she meant. The plain had been largely featureless, a foggy desert, but the foot of the mountain at close view was covered with fungoid brilliance. What had seemed like bare stone was actually gray and blue fungus, its hugely spreading tops an umbrella over the lesser growths. What appeared to be sand was the salt and pepper of myriad tiny spokes emerging from a brown spongelike underpinning. Between were layered colors—red, yellow, blue and black, the individual plants shaped like funnels, horns, brackets, plates and, yes, toadstools. From a distance it was all a blur, largely the fault of the atmosphere; close, it was a wonderland of shape and color. He pulled to a halt.

"Don't touch anything," he warned her. "Some of these mushrooms could be poisonous." Then he felt foolish, remembering her training; she should be warning *him*. There was no danger of anyone taking a bite.

Aquilon unfolded a tripod from her pad and painted busily. She wore brown shorts and a white blouse and filled both so well Veg found it hard to look at her. He wondered again why she had deserted the popular life she could have had on Earth to venture into lonely space. But she offered no hint, as she twirled her brush and duplicated item after item in full color.

He walked to the rear of the tractor and lifted the catch on the back equipment hold. There, suspended in a comprehensive padded harness, was a very small, thin, bespectacled man with sparse brown hair. His trousers and sleeves were full length, as though he did not want people to see his limbs, and his shirt came together in a snug collar about a small neck.

"How you doing, Cal?"

The little man smiled bravely. "Well enough," he said, but his face was pinched and white.

"We stopped to draw some pictures," Veg explained. "Maybe you want a few samples?"

The sunken eyes brightened. "You found some distinctive varieties!" The emaciated hands came up to touch the fastenings of the harness, then dropped wearily. "Perhaps you could select a few for me."

"Sure," Veg said, embarrassed. He could see that the ride had been hard on his friend. He kept forgetting that others did not always share his enthusiasm for speed. Cal had not adapted properly to the gravity of Nacre, though it was less than that of Earth, and the filters impeded his breathing. In space, under null-gravity conditions, he was all right, and he had a liquid suspension bath for conditions of acceleration. On land—he suffered. But Cal was Cal, and had insisted on coming on the exploratory excursion, rough as the journey might be. He was as excited as Aquilon about what might lie in the mountain range. It was not courage he lacked, but strength.

Veg donned protective gloves and marched toward the most luxuriant display. "Not those!" Aquilon cried, startling him into drawing a breath through his mouth. Her voice was apt to do that to him. He expelled the air hastily, realizing that she wanted to preserve that particular group for a portrait, and moved over.

The atmosphere of Nacre had been exhaustively tested and pronounced safe—in moderation. A few breaths through the mouth would not cause serious discomfort, and all personnel were trained to breathe automatically through the filters, even in sleep. Veg knew this, but the unfiltered air seemed unclean and it upset him to inhale it.

The flora and fauna were another matter. Some of these were deadly in unexpected ways, and most had yet to be tested and classified. The rule: Do not touch until the laboratory has taken apart and approved.

Aquilon glanced at him as he advanced upon the bend of the outcropping, but he did not interrupt her sketching. Veg stopped, spread out a collection sheet, and carefully reached out to grip the nearest offerings.

The fungi were even fancier than he had thought, and so thickly packed that there was no clear way to isolate them for individual harvest. Yellow goo flowed where his feet had crushed minute growths, and he regretted this accidental destruction. He reached for an Earth-sky-blue six-inch stinkhorn, afraid the projecting tip would break off and crumble in his hand, but to his relief and surprise it was as solid as a stick of wood. He worked it free, sadly snipping off the wirelike root strands, and laid it on the cloth.

Farther along was a specimen about the size of a

softball, with innumerable spaghetti-like threads twisting about. These moved as his hand approached, startling him. He jerked back, almost losing his balance, and glanced over the outcropping of mushroom-rock into the alcove beyond.

He stiffened. " 'Quilon," he called in a low tone.

She knew immediately that something important was there. She came swiftly and quietly and followed the direction of his gaze. "I see it," she said, as tense and quiet now as he.

It was a bay in the sea of dust, and squatting in front of a smaller inlet was a creature about the size of a small crouched man. From this vantage point the most distinctive feature was its enormous single eye.

"What is it?" she asked him. Veg did not reply. The creature stood unmoving, its eye, three inches across, focused unwaveringly upon them. The body was hunched into a globular mass balanced upon a single muscular foot.

They exchanged glances. Veg shook his head at the unspoken question. "We're only supposed to note the lay of the land," he said. "We don't dare mess with the local life—not something as strange as this."

"It doesn't look dangerous."

"But eighteen men were killed before we arrived— by something. . . ." He did not need to say more. They were conditioned to caution as members of a semiprivate troubleshooting expedition investigating a promising but dangerous planet. Pay was to some extent contingent upon success in solving the problem, and qualified volunteers were scarce. Strange people enlisted and strange things happened—but individuals avoided risks not so much for personal safety as from consideration for the needs of the expedition. A foolishly brave man was a liability.

Veg had wondered from time to time why Cal was allowed to stick with the group, since he was most apt to get himself killed. Perhaps it was because he was also most apt to put his finger, feeble as it might be, directly upon the source of trouble, and thus save many other lives and much time.

At any rate, they were bound to watch this strange creature, but not to approach it, however much they might be tempted to.

Aquilon was already sketching, wasting no motions. Color flowed from her brush, seemingly of its own volition. She flicked it, once, at Veg; a bright red dab flew to spatter against his cheek. Satisfied, she returned to her picture, the magic strokes quickly evoking a lifelike image of the animal ahead.

"Got a tail," Veg said, wiping at his face with good humor, "but no jaws. Not like the omnivore. How does it fight?"

She did not comment, rapidly filling new sheets of canvasite. All the animals they had observed on Nacre—and there were not many—were constructed on a roughly similar blueprint, as though radiating from a common ancestor. Just as the animals of Earth had settled on four limbs and two eyes, regardless of the vertebrate species, those of Nacre stayed with one foot and one eye. But, as on Earth, these animals diverged into large and small, bold and shy, predator and prey. The most savage of them all was the omnivore.

"Could have weapons that don't show," Veg said,

having nothing to do while Aquilon painted. "That eye—"

Even from this distance the eye was impressive. It glittered from a convex surface like a lens, as deep and dark as a well. Inside, perhaps just beyond the visible spectrum, there seemed to be a flicker, almost a glow.

". . . something about it," Aquilon agreed, sketching an enlarged view of the organ.

Veg drew her back at last, his two hands on her slender shoulders while she continued to paint. "We'd better get home and report this thing. Might be important."

She acquiesced reluctantly. They backed away until the creature was hidden from view behind the projecting arm of the mountain; then Veg stood guard while Aquilon ran to the tractor to explain the situation to Cal. Veg kept his hand on his sidearm, hoping he would not have to draw it. For one thing, he never liked using a weapon, though he did when he had to; for another, he had no guarantee that the repellant fog it emitted would be effective, since this creature was quite different from any seen before.

After allowing Aquilon time, he backed the rest of the way to the tractor. He had been careless to harvest mushrooms without checking the area thoroughly first. The thing could have crept upon them silently. . . .

"That's all I got," he said apologetically to Cal as he deposited the single fungus and closed up the compartment. The little man only nodded, and Veg knew he was wishing he had been able to see the new creature. A single glance would mean more to

Cal than ten minutes to Veg. "I'll glide by it as we go. You can watch through your periscope."

"If only radio worked on this planet—" Aquilon complained as he joined her in the front. It was a familiar grumble; parties did not like being out of contact with the main base, but the dust seemed to blank out most electromagnetic radiation in the atmosphere. Later, alternative communication would be worked out; but now they had to desert a phenomenal discovery because they could not summon another party from the base. "We may never see it again."

He started the huge motors and ground slowly forward. The vehicle rounded the edge of the mountain and cut into the bay.

The animal remained, flickering inscrutably. Veg drew carefully opposite, then stopped and turned, hoping Cal was getting a satisfactory view. The man was fascinated by extraterrestrial life of all kinds, but especially by the larger animals. This would make his day.

The tractor spun to face its own retreating spoor. Aquilon, still curious, mounted the back of the seat to watch over the top of the vehicle as they departed. Veg glanced once at the several square inches of soft thigh exposed, then bit his lip and concentrated upon his driving. His expression was thoughtful.

The creature moved. Veg could see it in the rear vision screen. It made an awkward, high leap, twisting in the air to land on its foot a dozen feet nearer the tractor. The lambent alien eye still watched intently.

"I think it's as curious about us as we are about

it," Aquilon said brightly, still facing behind as they picked up speed. "It's following us."

Veg grinned, relieved now that the three were safely in the moving machine. "Maybe it wants to race." He accelerated to an even twenty miles per hour. "Let me know when it gives up."

"Not yet," the girl said. She watched the creature leap and leap again, approaching the tractor, while Veg watched her watching. "It's catching up to us."

Veg grunted and played with the controls, letting out the mighty engine until the indicator registered thirty-five.

"It's still gaining," Aquilon said, genuinely excited now and even more attractive in that condition. "But —it isn't the same. I mean—" She faltered and glanced at him as though expecting a rebuke. "It—I think it changed its shape. To hop faster."

This was no overstatement, as he could see for himself. The body had flattened out and elongated, and the bounding effect was gone. The foot had become a pistonlike pushing member, touching the ground at intervals of twenty feet, sending the body forward in long shallow trajectories. The large eye was in the front of a head now tapered like a rocket, fading back into a neckless trunk, and the long tail streamed behind.

Veg tried to watch screen, girl and the view ahead, but had to alternate. "We latched on to something here," he muttered, rising to the challenge. "But if it really wants to race—"

Once more the tractor accelerated. It had been built for high speed over rough terrain, and was as potent a machine as Earth produced. Veg switched on the headlights and maneuvered deftly around the rapidly looming fungi. Aquilon hung on to the hand rail behind the seat as the thick wind tore at her body. Her blouse inflated and hair shot over her face in a rigid bonnet. She faced back still, a look of solemn excitement on her comely features, lips parted but breathing through her nose, intent on the uniped behind. At sixty it began, slowly, to fall away.

Aquilon reluctantly lowered herself down into the seat, fighting the fierce currents and jolts. "I never saw anything so fast—" She realized only then that her blouse had torn free of the elastic waistband and now hung loosely over shoulders and arms.

Veg nodded appreciatively but made no comment. He wasn't going to get her mad at him again!

She tucked herself together and leaned over to view the screen before the driver. "Look!"

Directly behind, the creature was gaining again.

Veg's mouth dropped open. "But we're doing seventy-five!" he protested.

Aquilon watched closely, while Veg peered in frustration past her head. He did not really have the time to concentrate on the screen at this velocity. He was approaching the limit of forward visibility under Nacre conditions, and Cal would not be appreciating the roughness of the ride.

"It changed again," she said, a little smugly, and described it to him. The thing no longer leaped or pushed at all; instead it stayed close to the ground, its foot moving so rapidly that it was invisible at contact. The body moved on an almost level course, flattened all the way into a thin disk ten feet in diameter. The vast front eye still stared ahead, hypnotic, glowing darkly.

"How could I have thought it awkward?" Aquilon whispered. "It's the most beautiful thing, like a butterfly—no, like a swimming manta ray, back on Earth. Only it swims in the *air,* so swift—"

The tractor leaped forward, its motors roaring. "This time," Veg said with grim enthusiasm, "this time I'm *really* going to show it dust!" He touched a button and an armored canopy slid over the cockpit, killing the turbulence within. But heavy vibration jarred the occupants as the vehicle sped over the plain in a straight course, blasting apart the mists and shattering the fungi in its path. He was proud of the machine, with its engine composed of a motor for every wheel and its overwhelming impetus.

The thick dust stirred at last, obscuring the afterview, and once again the pursuer was lost to sight. But in a moment it reappeared, off to the side and still gaining over the tractor's speed of ninety-five.

"Is there any limit?" Aquilon breathed, staring raptly at it. "Such a performance . . ."

As the tractor continued to accelerate, the flat thing outside slowly forfeited ground, and was finally lost again in the mists. This time it did not return.

Veg eased off slowly, somewhat intoxicated by the speed. He seldom had a pretext to really push the tractor.

Aquilon was first to react, lifting her flaxen head like an alert doe. "Burning," she said. "Something is burning!"

Veg laughed and pinched her bare knee with corded fingers. Then he smelled it. "Oh-oh."

The tractor slued alarmingly. "Wheel's froze up," he grunted. "Got to cut that motor. Damn dust must've—"

It lurched again, throwing them both to one side. Veg cursed and fought the controls; Aquilon unplastered her bosom from his shoulder and braced herself against the opposite corner. The dust ascended in surging clouds, hiding earth and sky.

The sturdy vehicle did not topple. They sat quietly while the pocket storm outside subsided, then choked jointly as the reek of well-charred insulation fumed in. Veg released the canopy and forced it back by hand. The incoming swirl of dust washed out the bitter air and gave their filters something tangible to work on.

"We're stranded," Veg said bluntly. "Own fault. This machine won't move for weeks."

Aquilon worked it out for herself. "In this mist and dust there won't be any tracks to follow by the time they realize we're lost ... and we can't signal them. A full search pattern would take too long."

There was a groan. Her eyes widened. "We forgot Cal!"

Veg banged the door open and jumped to the ground. Aquilon slid over and dismounted more carefully. Together, they circled through the settling particles to the rear of the tractor.

Cal's glasses were broken and hooked over one ear, but there was no blood on his face. Veg unfastened the harness and lifted him down.

Aquilon flung both arms about the unconscious man and held him up while Veg checked his body quickly for injuries. "He's okay," he announced "Spinout must've made him light-headed." He hoped he was right.

Aquilon set Cal on the ground and cradled his head upon her thighs. Before long his eyes opened.

"There appears to have been a—shake-up," he murmured.

Veg relaxed, only now allowing himself to admit how worried he had been. The shock could have thrown his friend into a coma, and if there had been any internal injury—"a shake-up! Friend, if *I* woke up in a lap like that, I'd be shook up, and I'd damn well think of something better to say than—!" He was compensating for his concern by showing mock gruffness.

Cal smiled but Aquilon did not. Veg turned away, irked yet again by his seeming ability to say the wrong thing. They all knew that his little jokes were just thinly veiled appeals for—

For what? For the same thing the spaceport professionals provided for pay or glamor? Was he that hard up already, that he had to chase after the friend of his friend? And if by some mischance he got her—would she then be no more to him than those contemptible others? Aquilon was a nice girl. What demon prompted him to dream of destroying her?

"Spores," Cal said, sitting up with Aquilon's help.

"Spores?" For a moment Veg was afraid Cal's mind *had* been affected.

"This is a fungus world—insufficient light for chlorophyll plants, on the ground, at any rate. Much of this 'dust' is in reality a surplus mass of spores, microscopically small, since that is the way most fungi reproduce. A palynologist will tell you that you could fit fifty sextillion of them in a level teaspoon. They float in the air and get into everything, and there are so many types that even on Earth they are constantly feeding on new materials. Probably some worked into the wheel bearings and sprouted in the oil, leading to—"

Cal was back to normal.

Veg moved over to stand before a locker in the side of the tractor. He stared silently into the interior, frowning.

"Supplies?" Aquilon inquired. Her head, as she came to stand beside him, barely passed his shoulder.

"Steam rifle and a compass," he said with disgust. "We're in trouble, Beautiful."

She ducked under his arm and poked into the compartment. "It's a complete survival pack," she said, pleased. "Knives, matches, first aid, handbook. . . . We can hike back to the base, with this."

Veg studied her.

"Why look," she continued innocently. "The compass shows only twenty-four miles. That's not so far—" She broke off, noticing that Veg wasn't responding. "What's the matter?"

"I never met a woman yet who could think straight. That score miles is straight cross-country; follow level ground, it's more like a hundred. We were a couple of hours out, in the tractor. You and I, 'Quilon, might make it. . . ."

"Oh." Her hand flew to her mouth. "Cal. . . ."

"Yeah." Veg got to work unloading the compartment and setting up the knapsack provided.

Already a thin film of the ubiquitous powder falling naturally had formed on the horizontal surfaces of the vehicle. Only the ghostly, dead white fungus giants interrupted the obscurity of the shrouded plain. It was not cold, but Veg saw Aquilon shiver as he tightened the pack, picked up the rifle, and took his bearing from the compass.

"Couldn't you cut across by yourself and bring help?" she asked without particular hope. "You could make it in a day and we'd be safe in the tractor."

"If I knew the terrain, yes," Veg said seriously. "But there are some bad drop-offs around, worse because you can't see 'em. The camp sits right under a cliff. If something happened to me, or even if I were delayed only a little, you'd be finished. With only one real weapon, no food and precious little water, we can't split up." He chucked her under the chin, trying to break the mood. "Besides, I want you where I can keep an eye on you." He pointed across the fog. "That way—and pray it stays level after all. Help the lady, Cal."

Aquilon caught the hint and took hold of the little man's elbow. They moved out, following Veg's lead. The pace was slow—hardly two miles an hour, but Cal stumbled almost immediately. He had discarded the useless glasses, but that was only part of the problem; he could see well enough at intermediate range, and wouldn't need to read on the journey. Sweat beaded his brow as he struggled to advance, but it was evident that even this slow pace was too much for his wasted body.

The woman, half a head taller than he and heavier, put her arm around his waist firmly and half-lifted him, helping him forward. Cal grimaced at the pressure of her arm but did not speak. Veg, rifle ready and eyes scanning the trek facing them, tried not to look back, but he slowed his pace until a balance was struck.

Two hours later they hove in sight of a group of animals. "Herbivores," Veg said. "No danger."

"Food," Aquilon said. "Why don't we wait here while you bring back a small one? We could use the break." She meant that Cal could use it, principally.

Veg started to say something, then changed his mind. She had forgotten; that was all. Still, he could bring back a live one for her. . . . He slung the pack to the ground and headed for the herd at a rapid pace, still wearing the rifle.

Over twenty miles to go! He could make it so easily . . . and so could Aquilon. But Cal—

The trouble was they could not do it at Cal's pace. That would take three days at least, with the frequent rests, and while they might last that long without food, the lack of water would bring them down. He was thirsty already, and there was only a quart bottle of sterile water, intended for first-aid use. They would drink that, of course—but for how long?

Sooner or later it would occur to Cal that he was impeding their chances. Then there would really be trouble. Veg had no intention of deserting his friend. He would simply have to carry him; maybe that way they could make good enough time. Aquilon could carry the pack. He'd have to strip it down, throw out everything they weren't sure they'd need. . . .

He kicked at a football-sized fungus bulging out of a crevice in the dust. It held its ground and absorbed his boot spongily, almost tripping him. Veg cursed and recovered his balance, as angry at himself for taking out his passion on an innocuous living thing as at it for resisting the blow. There was transparent moisture dripping from his toe; he had wounded it after all. He went on, nagged by something but unable to place it, quite.

He approached the edge of the herd, not bothering to unstring the rifle. The peaceful herbivores of Nacre were common, and no threat to anyone. Their flesh *was* edible, but he did not propose to slaughter one, not even for Aquilon. She would have to do that herself—and he didn't think she would.

Like virtually all the animals here, these were one-legged. He could see several hopping about, covering two or three feet with each effort. Racers they were not; they did not travel much, and a herd migrated only gradually in much the same manner as a dune of sand: one particle at a time. There were about fifty members here, and no more than half a dozen were moving, seeking fresher pasture at the forward edge. The others were grazing, their long pink breathing gills extending from the tops of their knoblike heads to give individuals a faintly rabbity appearance. The group, inspected as a whole, resembled a field of gently waving grain. He had heard that those gills extracted water, among other things, from the atmosphere; too bad human beings couldn't do that!

The herbivores came in all colors of gray and all sizes of medium and grew, as nearly as had been determined, for life. A few were taller than himself and somewhat more massive. He stooped to pick up a medium-small representative that looked as though it weighed no more than fifty pounds. He had had contact with these creatures before, but had never quite overcome his amazement at the complete alienness of them.

He put his hands on this one's narrowest part,

catching it just above the circular foot before it could realize what he was doing and hop away. He heaved. It came up easily, making no sound. The foot, splayed in a full circle to feed on the nutrient dust, flopped loosely as he lifted the creature into the air and held it before him.

The globular body rose in a hump like that of an octopus, and the single eye bulged placidly. The long breathing gill flowered at an angle now, an undulating mass of fine fibers.

The waving antenna brushed his face with a damp and gentle touch, and through it he saw Aquilon coming up to the herd. "Your pet!" he shouted, knowing that the noise would not disturb these creatures; no animal so far discovered on Nacre made any vocal noise or possessed hearing apparatus. It was a silent planet—which, as Cal had pointed out, was strange, because the perpetual mist made sight a far less useful perception than it was elsewhere. The falling dust inhibited light and damped out beams and signals of any—

The distance between himself and Aquilon had halved, and she was waving her arms and shouting. "Veg! Behind you!"

He whirled, still holding the herbivore. Something bounded out of the herd, rising far too high to be a normal member of its company. Sleek and black, its body contrasted sharply with the gray shades of its neighbors, too. A great eye shone from the thing, unnaturally malignant and totally unlike the empty mirrors of the herbivores. It landed at the edge of the group nearest Veg and moved toward him, flattening into a suddenly familiar shape.

"The manta!" Aquilon screamed.

Veg dropped his burden and slid the rifle into one hand with an experienced twitch of the shoulder. This was the last thing he had expected, and he felt naked in the presence of such a menace. A race in the tractor had been one thing; but to meet it in the open—

The heat chamber of his rifle flared as it built up pressure. His hands had been doing the right things automatically, as though they were more eager to kill than he was. It only took a few seconds for the steam to form—seconds that seemed very long, right now—but after that the rifle was good for service limited only by the aim of the marksman and the quantity of ammunition.

The manta came, shimmying toward the side, incredibly fast. Now he saw the whiplike tail, and with a sick insight he realized what that tail could do. He hadn't wanted to fire, but there was no longer a choice.

The steam hissed as he squeezed the trigger: once, twice. The manta came on, unhurt. Cursing, Veg ripped an explosive shell from the stock and clapped it into the auxiliary chamber. He held back another moment, however, despising the shell as, at best, unsporting.

The manta was little more than a thin line, head on, moving now at such a velocity that it was over Veg before he could aim properly the second time. It passed a foot above his head—but did not strike.

Now it landed between him and Aquilon, facing her. Veg saw her recoil in terror from its immense disk, she who had thought it so beautiful, with the trailing tail and the great eye that seemed to plummet through its entire length. It was after her!

Veg fired. This time the manta shook as the shell tore open its body. It spun, coalescing in mid-air, then fell heavily and moved no more.

He had killed it after all.

II. A Jug of Wine

THE MOUNTAINS GAVE way to the northern lakelands as Subble guided his flyer west, avoiding the crowded airspace above Appalachia. Then he cut south across the antipollutant smokestacks of the Midwest and angled on into the flat expanse of the intensive farmland beyond the Mississippi. Juggernauts trod along the endless plantations like mighty harvester ants, far too powerful to be challenged by barehanded man yet militant in the protection of the tenderest shoot of corn.

He drifted across the massed elevated pipelines of the rapidly depleting Oklahoma oilfields and landed at last upon one of the towering residentials just north of the Texas border. There was ample parking space on the broad asphalt roof of the address in his notes, and he taxied to the visitor's lot without event. A conveyor took him to the nearest elevator. The layout was standard, if unimaginative; so far everything was routine.

He stepped out on the twentieth floor down and navigated the cubistic maze until he found the proper apartment. The door opened promptly to his summons and warm air puffed out. A strikingly beautiful woman stood before him, the image of the girl of

Nacre come stunningly to life in the long skirts and low bodice of a pseudo-gypsy siren. Her long fair hair was carelessly looped in a crude knot, as though tied in a preoccupied hurry, but this could not detract appreciably from the classic lines of her face. She was blue-eyed and barefooted and gently smiling.

"You are—"

"'Quilon," she said immediately. "Come in. I need you."

Subble entered, picking up the spring essence of the simple perfume she wore. His perceptions told him that this woman was far more complicated and disturbed than Veg had seen her, but not dangerous in the physical sense. She was in many ways complimentary to the bluff, powerful vegetarian, and it was not strange that they were in love.

"I am—"

"One of those agents," she said. She handed him a folded stack of material. "Put this on, please."

Subble withdrew to her tiny bedroom and changed, setting his inconspicuous trousers and jacket carefully upon her bed. He did not worry about the things she might discover therein; only a trained weaponist would recognize the subtle modifications in cloth and leather, and in any event he would keep alert.

She had provided him with an archaic, outlandish space costume of the type reputed to have been employed during the earliest days of space exploration: cumbersome, heavy cloth and a bulbous transparent helmet. This *was* a costume, however, and hardly mistakable for anything else; the cloth was porous and the helmet fashioned of fiberglass mesh.

"Good," she said as he emerged. "Now stand before that backdrop and look tired. You're supposed to be the second man on the moon, back in the 1970's, lost in the shadow fringe with the sun coming up. You have to find shelter in six hours or less or Sol will fry you. That's good."

She had set up an easel and was half-hidden behind a large canvasboard. Her right hand flirted with color and image while her left guided him by signals into the exact posture she desired.

"Turn your handsome face away from me—down a little—bend your knees—more—good. Hold it there," she said. "Now you can talk, or whatever it is you came to do, so long as you don't violate the pose."

"You do commercial illustration," Subble said, not moving.

"At the moment," she agreed. "But I paint all the time, whether I expect to be paid for it in money or not."

"You receive payment other than money?" Though she had positioned him so that he could not watch her now, his ears and nostrils kept him informed of her exact position and mood. Her breathing was slightly irregular, her heart-beat accelerated, and the perfume could not conceal the odors of nervousness emanating from her. She was not nearly as sure of herself as she wanted him to believe.

"The best," she said. "Peace of mind." But she was far from such reward at the moment. "What do you want with me?"

"I'm not certain."

She laughed. "It is a strange man who says that to me! But that's right—they make you learn every-

thing for yourself, don't they? To keep you on your
. . . toes. I should think that would be dangerous,
though."

"We are equipped for it."

She was more at ease now, as though she had
scored a point. "I can see that. You hold that pose as
though you're a statue. Not even a quiver. It takes a
very special control to do that. But suppose someone
simply refused to talk to you?"

"I can still learn much of what I need to. But I'd
much prefer to have cooperation."

She was nervous again. "Change into this," she
said, bringing him another costume.

Subble returned to her room and switched outfits.
He noted that she had none of her own paintings on
display here, and nowhere were there any depicting
Nacre.

The new costume was a conservative twentieth-
century business suit, the sole incongruous note a
bright campaign button pinned to the right lapel
proclaiming LET'S BACK JACK!

Aquilon had also changed, and stood in a head-
to-toe scuba-diving rig that appeared to be genuine.
The clinging rubberized suit displayed a figure that
required no enhancement. She was one of the health-
iest, loveliest women of the times, judged by his
objective standards. It was unusual for such a creature to bury herself alone.

"This is for a period 'confession' reprint," she
said. "You just stand there full-face and look interested, as though about to fall desperately in love
with a sweet girl. No, *not* lascivious. *Interested.* You
see her as the ideal homemaker, wife and—No." She
tucked her brush behind her right ear and stepped

from behind the canvasboard. "Look at me. I am the future mother of your children, but you aren't in love with me yet. It's all potential. Raise your eyebrows a little, put one hand searchingly forward, fingers curved but relaxed, your weight on the balls of your feet but a trifle overbalanced as though you are about to take a step. Yes." She took a breath which further defined her remarkable bosom. "Now imagine me in a kitchen apron, ironing your shirts. This is 1960, you know; everything has to be ironed. It all has to show on your face, right down to the year and the season. Spring, of course. You know what they say: the desire of the man is for the woman, but the desire of the woman is for the desire of the man. But it has to be *clean* desire. This is a clean publication. You have to be the type of man whose desire the nice girl desires, if you see what I mean. There! Hold that expression."

She painted industriously. "Now show me how you're going to get information from an uncooperative client," she said, her voice suddenly drained of animation. She, like Veg, demanded personal proof.

Subble watched her and discovered the trap. The board concealed the main portion of her torso, so that he could not directly observe the variations in her breathing and posture, and the opaque suit covered possible skin flushes and minute muscular reactions, as well as sealing in bodily odors. She lowered a tinted plastic face mask and breathed through a functioning oxygen system, so that there were no hints there either. He could still see her face—but it was as expressionless as a photograph.

Aquilon knew about special agents.

"Very nice," he said. "But the very fact you can

turn off your facial animation gives me a starting point, and even if I had no other sources I could learn much by studying your apartment. If the need were urgent, I could strip you and so reestablish the physical signals. That would be interesting enough— they'd have to assign the competition handicaps if you entered a beauty contest. But I repeat: I want only what you will give me freely."

She lifted the mask. "Information, you mean."

"Certainly."

"I wonder. Is it true that you are wiped out after each mission?"

"It is true."

"Isn't that like dying?"

"No. It's like freedom from dying."

She shuddered expressively, no longer bothering to control her physical reactions. "Why? I mean, what harm can a few memories do?"

"A great deal. The point is that we are virtually alike—every single agent—except for slight superficial variations in skin color, weight, fingerprints, and so on. That's to avoid the appearance of duplication and lessen notoriety. We are almost identical where it counts, in mind, physique and training. If an agent were permitted to retain individual experiences, he would shortly *become* an individual, and the objectivity of uniformity would be sacrificed."

"But some memories might help you do the next job better."

"Such memories are erased from the individuals, then implanted uniformly in the entire corps."

She flushed. "You mean if the computer thought you should remember me it would put me in thousands of minds? And every single agent in the world would know where I lived and . . . everything?"

He smiled reassuringly. "It could—"

"That's it! That's the expression."

He held it while she completed her portrait, then went on. "The computer *could* spread you across the globe, but it is unlikely that it would deem so unusual a woman as yourself to be suitable material for that. You can safely assume that our personal relationship is private."

"I'll have to," she muttered. "Change again."

This time it was a scant jungle-man costume, hardly more than a loin cloth. He had to dangle from a fixture set in the ceiling, by one hand, while holding aloft a papier-mâché "club" with the other. Aquilon had also changed again, to an Asiatic toga.

"Try to look as though you're swinging on a vine," she said. Then, as an afterthought: "You do have nice musculature."

"All part of the specifications, ma'am."

She painted. "Do they let you *live* between assignments? Or is it all work and no play?"

"We are given breaks after completing each mission," Subble said. "There are generally a number of agents of both sexes in the termination pool. But we *live*, as you put it, all the time. We encounter some fascinating people in the line of duty." He was still hanging.

"But you can't *keep* it," she said. "They might as well line you up before a firing squad. And you *know* extinction is coming."

"On the contrary. No need to italicize your words at *me*, miss. I told you before that we are free from dying. You look ahead to a tedious gradual aging and loss of faculties and inevitable sickness and death. That is a lifelong dying. I look forward only to a completed mission and a paid vacation. I don't have to worry about age or disability, or even be concerned about the future. Death is not a spectre to me. I know that all of my conscious life I will be a virtual superman facing the world's most intriguing challenges. The best of any life is reserved for me."

"Do you realize you've been hanging by one arm for six minutes?"

"Five minutes, thirty-five seconds at the mark," he said. "Mark."

She looked at her watch. "You *are* quite a man. You can let go now."

Subble dropped noiselessly to the floor. "Technically, I'm not a man, in that sense. I'm a number. I'm identified by a three-letter code, SUB, with a humanizing suffix. I differ from SUA or SUC or SUD no more than my code does."

"I don't believe it," she said, nettled. "You must have feelings."

"Not on duty. After this mission is over, I will have a few days to remember you and your friend Veg and appreciate your doubtless charming individual qualities. But at the moment—"

"Oh," she said, rising to the challenge. "So you have no normal human reactions right now. No pleasure, no anger, no. . . ?"

"I have them, but they are completely controlled."

She was silent a few seconds. "I have to do a series for a 'Nature' magazine. The law doesn't allow it through the fax, but it still has a fair mechanical circulation. Just toss your Tarzan suit over there."

"You are asking me to pose naked?"

"Unless you have human scruples." She poised her brush before a new canvas expectantly.

Subble removed the loincloth.

Aquilon stared at him for thirty seconds before speaking. "This will illustrate the cover of an issue with a guaranteed circulation of four hundred and twenty thousand," she said at last.

"Agents have appeared on covers before."

"You go this far—just to obtain the answers to a few questions?"

"An agent will do anything within reason to maintain a harmonious relationship and uphold the integrity of the service. My body is public property, and you appear to have a valid use for it. Once you have confidence in me, perhaps you will no longer wish to withhold the information I need."

"Put your arms forward as though about to dive into a pool," she said. "Give me a three-quarter view." Then, as he posed, she began to talk about herself. "It's a triangle. Veg and Cal and I—we're in love. I know that sounds funny. But I have to choose *one* of them, and I can't. I just can't make the decision. That's why we split up, mainly. It just wasn't possible, together, any more, in spite of—of what happened. I have to go to one of them—when I can." She paused apprehensively. "How much did Veg tell you?"

"That he loved you. That the three of you were marooned on Nacre. That he killed a 'manta.' "

"That was all? Just to the—"

"That was all. He felt that was his share, and that the rest belonged to you and Calvin."

"Yes . . ." She painted quietly for a while. "Well,

now I have to choose. I might make love with one, but then I'd have to do it with the other, too, to be fair. That would be promiscuity, and they'd both know it. I care too much for them both to hurt them like that. It's too intimate. I could sleep with someone I didn't care about, because that's only the body, public property, as you say. It's the emotion that counts. Who my heart sleeps with."

She paused again, studying him frankly. "I could sleep with you, the sexual part I mean, because I'm not involved with you. It would just be a physical release. An impersonal thing. Would you like that?"

"My preferences have no bearing on my duty."

"So if I offered myself to you, physically, right now, you'd decline?"

"Unless there were legitimate contrary reason, yes."

"Legitimate reason!"

"Do you wish me to continue this pose?"

"No, but stay where you are. I want to know just how far this control of your extends." She touched her toga and it unwrapped languorously from her body. She wore nothing underneath. "Now take a good look at me."

Subble obliged. "Is comment required?"

She sighed. "You've proved your point, if that isn't an abysmal pun. You haven't been fooled at all, have you? You knew I meant to vamp you, to avoid telling you about Nacre."

"Veg tried to use his fists."

"With equivalent success, I'm sure. And Cal will use his mind. And you'll absorb it all unmoved and complete your assignment on schedule."

"I have no schedule. I was impressed by Veg's

nature, as I am by yours. You should not mistake my physical control for disparagement."

She marched to her collection of costumes and tossed him a man's bathrobe. "Let's get drunk."

Dressed in HIS and HERS robes, they started for her kitchenette. She put out a hand. "Wait."

He waited.

She made her decision and turned about. "This way."

He followed her out the door and down the hall to the elevator. She punched for the basement forty stories below. The other passengers stared straight ahead, not deigning to notice the intimate dishabille: loose hair, bare legs and feet, matching bathroom attire—but Subble could pick up the remarks of those who got off. He smiled. The basement *did* seem like a peculiar destination for such a couple. . . .

The basement—actually, he was sure, the first of a number of unnumbered sublevels—was an austere compartment opening into several hallways. There was a directory billboard, but Aquilon ignored it. She led him down one of the central passages.

Pipes of tremendous girth crossed the low ceiling, and tunnellike offshoots led to pits with collections of valves and indicators. There was a light but pervasive aroma compounded of—he sniffed and isolated the principal components—mildew, animal dung, seed pellets, insecticide, ammonia, machine oil and offal. This would be the area's intensive livestock production unit; many residentials had their own, to avoid interstate controls, shipping charges and taxes.

One other smell: the same suggestion of alienness he had noted when searching for the vanishing trace of the thing in Veg's forest. The—creature had been here within a day. Was that why she had brought him here?

At the end of the hall a man sat at a desk poring over a chart. He looked up as they approached. He smiled. "Good to see you, 'Quilon," he said, rubbing his puffy eyes. Subble read the ingrained fatigue in him, the subdued desperation and misery. This man was unhappily married, sick of his job, bored and ridden with guilt. His pulse quickened as Aquilon came near him. He was not smitten with her, being too realistic for that, but he appreciated her physical qualities fiercely. He daydreamed, almost certainly, of an eventual liaison—but that was not the source of the guilt.

" 'Lo, Joe," Aquilon replied, and smiled. The man's expression did not change, but Subble picked up the electric glow that shot through his physique and vitalized him; he was a sucker for the attentions of a lovely woman, particularly one so suggestively garbed. Aquilon, obviously, was using him; her smile was a cynical, calculated thing, as though the current were controlled by rheostat—yet she was prepared to arouse and oblige his passions in a certain not unlikely circumstance. She, like Veg, had come to terms with certain necessities—whatever these might be. It would be necessary to find out why she was cultivating Joe, Subble realized; probably it did involve the alien presence. The thing was hiding here, and a report by this man could betray it. "I'd like to show my guest the farm, if it's all right."

Joe looked at Subble. "What's a government agent

doing here?" he demanded suspiciously. "We're inspected regularly. We're a top-classification unit."

"Please," Aquilon said gently, leaning over the desk. The man basked in her warmth, ready to yield her anything.

"But it's all in order," he said in a final defensive reflex as he returned to his chart.

They entered the unit—and the smell magnified tremendously. "He's really a computer programmer," she said as she led the way down a narrow, straw-lined corridor. "But they put him here because he was assigned to streamline the farm. He has to be thoroughly familiar with it before he can set up new flow charts. The distribution of feed, the percentage of calcium in the formula, the intensity of the light—the stock is sensitive to little things, and the program has to be modified for each unit or the profit ratio suffers." Her tone showed that she had little sympathy with the suffering profit ratio. "It's all automated, of course, so he's the only one on duty except for a mechanic, until he gets the job done. That makes him the veterinarian, now, even though he hasn't been trained for it. And he hates it."

Subble nodded. Such things were common. Programmers too often wound up in *outré* situations, as did agents. Yet the popular imagination clothed them both in glamor and, oddly, a certain concurrent dislike.

"These are our bunnies," she said.

They stood in a well-lighted room decked on either side with lined cages, the lowest set so close to the center that there was less than a yard to walk in. The second layer was set back a foot, and the third another foot, so that there was a good deal of space at head height, just under the swishing air-ducts. The room was not air-conditioned; these appeared to be oxygenating units only, and it was hot. The odor was stifling.

"These are the growing hutches," she explained. "See, they have no floors, just wire mesh so the droppings can fall through. The nesting boxes are more comfortable—they have solid plastic at the bottom and genuine bedding. How would you like to spend your life in one of these?"

Subble inspected the nearest cage at her direction. A conveyor-trough brought the nutrient pellets through and a drip-valve provided water. Another conveyor transported the descending dung away slowly. The cage was about four feet long and half as wide with clearance barely high enough for the occupants to assume a normal stance. Within it were a mother rabbit, pure white, and her litter of nine pink-eared babies.

"She has to raise twelve families in two years— then she goes to the slaughter herself," Aquilon said. "Her pelt will find its way into some man's hat, and her delicate flesh will be packaged as quality broiler. She will never see honest daylight, and her only moment of pleasure, if that's what it is, is when the buck covers her. *He* doesn't get much leisure—he gets fed strictly according to the number of does he services, and if he falters, that's the end."

She got ready to tell him something important, but balked and led him into another area. What was it that worried these people so? Veg had not been frightened for himself, and neither was Aquilon, but both *were* frightened by something.

"Antibiotics are put in their food, but still a lot

die in the cages. Flies get in somehow, and mold.
Fungus pops up everywhere, and it seems to mutate
so rapidly that they can't keep up with it."

"As on Nacre?"

The question disturbed her. "Sometimes I wish it
were. This is the henhouse."

Here the lights were low and red. Subble had no
difficulty, but Aquilon had to wait a moment while
her vision adjusted. "It's so they won't flutter about
and peck each other," she said. "Some are de-beaked
anyway, or given blinders; but with only four to a
cage there isn't too much trouble. It's all down to a
science. The music helps, too."

Sure enough: the speakers were playing Bach's
"Sheep May Safely Graze," as though sweet melo-
dies could add to the freshness of the eggs.

"They aren't sheep, they can't graze, and they
certainly aren't safe," Aquilon remarked sourly.

The strains and harmonies were incongruous in
the gloom and stink of the battery. The cages were
similar to those for the rabbits except that their mesh
floors were tilted to make the eggs roll into external
troughs where they were borne gently away.

"What do you think of it?" she inquired as they
proceeded to another room.

"Good, standard outfit," he said. "Seems as efficient as the state of the art can make it."

She went on in silence.

The slaughtering section was more active, though
also fully automated. The selected young chickens
were funnelled into cul-de-sacs, urged on by moving
brushes, where a machine looped cord about their
feet, lifted them squawking and fluttering, and
shackled them upside-down to an elevated conveyor-

rod. At the end of the line another machine caught their struggling heads and slit their throats. The blood spouted into yet another trough.

"They aren't even stunned first," Aquilon said, shuddering. "Because their flapping helps the blood flow out more quickly, or something. I tried to have Joe write a stunner into the program, and he wanted to, but he said he'd be fired if he tried to include anything that would increase the cost like that. He's trapped in this mess, just as we all are."

Subble nodded agreement, though the realities of the situation did not strike him as a moral issue. A slaughter operation was not suitable for a man with scruples about pain—but the fate of a worker fired for inefficiency was not a sanguine one.

"If they don't die soon enough," she continued tightly, "the scalding tank takes care of that detail. Or the defeatherer, or the eviscerator. Most of the chickens, I'm sure, are dead by the time they are packaged, anyway." She no longer tried to play down the irony. "Still, their lot is better than that of the calves or pigs."

Subble saw that she was quite upset about it. This was not what she had intended to show him originally, but the issue was a serious one with her. She must have looked for a place to hide the alien—and found this, then become concerned with the conditions she found in the farm.

"Let's get out of here," she said. She had changed her mind again, still hesitating to reveal the secret overtly, though she must have realized that he would become aware of it. What held her back?

Back in the apartment she washed convulsively and in full view, as though her body had been soiled by flying blood. "Do you understand, now?" she asked as she toweled arms and breasts and donned a new bathrobe.

He stripped and washed, knowing that she would find him contaminated if he did not. "Why you have not eaten meat or eggs in several months? No," he said, giving her a chance to explain it herself. She needed a case to argue before she could settle down.

"If we can do this to our animals today, what will we be doing to ourselves tomorrow?" she demanded. Her voice was bitter, her eyes becoming red. "Don't you see how close we are already? This whole district—one mass of hutches for people, tier upon tier, each one fed by piped-in pellets called groceries and cleaned by communally flushing toilets. Every mind distracted by standard-formula canned entertainment that someone has programmed so there won't be too much fuss. They have to give tranquilizing drugs to the chickens so they won't turn to cannibalism when they get too crowded in their dark unnatural habitat —and we have drugs too, don't we, so we can stand it all a little longer."

She walked jerkily to the kitchenette and brought out a quart bottle of gin. "Come, deaden your mind with me," she invited, pouring two four-ounce portions.

"It is no kinder in nature," Subble pointed out. "What man does in the effort to feed himself is only a more disciplined extension of—"

"I know," she exclaimed. "I know, I know! It's absolutely logical, this terrible cruelty. So we have to starve the little calves of iron so their meat will be white, and force naturally cleanly pigs to wallow in filth to save a few pennies. There's reason to it all—but where is the heart in it? Isn't there some better way than this?"

"Emotionalism doesn't help."

"As chickens to the slaughter," she declaimed, brandishing her empty glass, "so mankind to the Bomb! I'm *ready!* Just water me and breed me and pluck me and—"

"If it is any consolation, I understand that intensive farming is on the decline," Subble said, disturbed by her attitude. "The need to rework the programs is evidence of that. Synthetics are more efficient."

"It doesn't matter," she said, collapsing into despair. "I still can't stand to be a member of a species that brutalizes this way. Veg is right. I'm an—an omnivore."

"All of us must be what we are—and it is not entirely evil. There are redemptions, even glories. You know that."

"My mind, not my heart," she said, sipping at another glass. "Ignorance is not bliss. I never knew what I was, until Nacre. Now I wish I could undo it all—a lifetime of thoughtless evil. I wish I were back there, the three of us back on Nacre, to stay forever and ever." She changed the subject abruptly. "You know, Veg called us 'Beauty, Brains and Brawn'," she said, demure for the moment. "I think of it as physical, emotional and intellectual—except I have the order mixed up—well, you know. But really it's—do you know Omar Khayyám?"

"The eleventh century astronomer-poet? Contemporary and friend of Hasan the Assassin, who—"

"Stop it!" she said with flash ferocity. "I mean the *Rubaiyat*—the poetry. 'A Book of Verses underneath the Bough, A Jug of Wine, a Loaf of Bread—and Thou.' "

" 'Beside me singing in the Wilderness—Oh, Wilderness were Paradise enow!' That would be Edward FitzGerald's rendition, third edition, I believe."

She stared somberly at him. "You're getting even for all that posturing I made you do. All right, have your fun. What *is* the difference between editions?"

"According to the literal translation of Heron-Allen, the words are: 'I desire a little ruby wine and book of verses/ Just enough to keep me alive, and half a loaf is needful;/ And then, that I and thou should sit in a desolate place/ Is better than the kingdom of a sultan.' McCarthy had two prose variants, Whinfield an alternate, Graves another, and FitzGerald's own first and second editions differed somewhat. Do you wish them quoted?"

"Why didn't you become an English teacher? You certainly have the touch for ruining something beautiful!" But her desolate mood had been broken.

"There may at some time be occasion to impersonate such a person. But more importantly, familiarity with literature, among other things, can lead to better comprehension of the key aspects of a complex situation. So we are educated rather carefully in this respect."

"The way my knowledge of anatomy helps me as an artist?"

"Something like that."

"Well, just don't try that stuff on Cal. He'll stand you on your literary head before you get the whole quotation out."

"I'll remember," he said, smiling.

She was on her third unadulterated glass. "As

soon as I saw your face," she murmured into it, "I knew what you were and what you wanted. But it isn't as simple as you think. No, I don't suppose you care whether it's simple or not. But this is—well, I just can't tell you what it is. Maybe if I drink enough I'll tell you. Maybe you'll have to make love to me after all to make me tell. You could force yourself, I'm sure. Maybe I'll just kill myself."

"Are you willing to show me the paintings?"

She looked at him sharply. "*What* paintings?"

"The ones you don't have on your bedroom wall."

"What's the use," she said, plopping an ice sphere into her gin. "He was bound to think of that. He's an agent." She stood up unsteadily and went to a locked closet, rummaging in her purse for the key. "I haven't shown these to anyone."

She brought several large canvases to the table, propping them against its leg. She held up the first. "That's the herbie herd," she said. "I repainted from my field notes."

Subble studied it with interest. Aquilon had great talent, and her heart and soul had gone into this painting.

The landscape presented was dark: the misty world of Nacre, named for its brightness in space and not from the surface denied that light. The bloated fungi Veg had described loomed in the background. In the foreground was the herd: standing blobs like squid with their tentacles fused into fleshy columns. The pink gills were so finely drawn they seemed to wave.

But it was the technique that touched him more than the fidelity to an alien landscape. Somehow Aquilon had put emotion into this painting and

78

made it live. It stirred him far more than her earlier
nudity had, for this was genuine and without affectation. He glanced at her with a respect he had not felt
before.

She brought up the second item: a smaller sheet
glued to a board. "This is the original," she said. "I
did it on the mountain ledge after the first day's
hike."

Subble did not remind her that this had not been
in the segment Veg had reported. "You paint when
you're tired?"

"I paint *because* I'm tired," she said quietly. Her
speech was becoming slow as the alcohol reached it.
"How else can I show my feelings?"

She reached for the bottle again, but Subble
caught her hand. "I'd rather you didn't," he said.
"Alcohol has little effect on me because my subconscious is aligned with my conscious. There are no
barriers to break down. But you—"

"What, *feelings* now? What do you care what I
do?"

Subble did not reply immediately. He contemplated the picture, thinking of the circumstances of
its creation. They must have been climbing, and
Aquilon dead tired, for she had had to help Cal.
Unable to relieve her feelings in normal expression,
she had turned to her painting. Her eyes had focused
on the phantom darkening gray of the sky while her
brush formed a scene. The painting, though done on
the spot, had to be from memory or imagination, for
the haze, formed from the microscopic debris of the
helio-animalcules high in the atmosphere—this much
he understood about the planet—combined with the
closing dusk to obscure everything more than a few

feet from the open ledge. But it had taken shape steadily: an image of the trail those three had covered in the last hour, creeping around the corners of the mountain, fungus clinging like stylized puffs of cotton.

The trail over which they had traveled would have been tortuous and ugly, and Aquilon's rendition of it was striking. Her picture was a composite of all the features of the climb. The fatigue of the steep ascent was there, and the hardness of bare rock; the nausea of tired feet skidding on the slime of crushed fungus. There was a hint of the hopelessness of a man who lacked the strength or the will to live, and perhaps also that of a girl who would not, then, smile.

But the painting itself was magnificent.

And had she then set it aside, on that far world, and leaned back against the vertical stone wall rising from the inner ledge? The pale blue rock of the mountain she depicted would have contrasted gently with the dark haze of the sky beyond the drop-off, and here, ringed by the billowing white fungus, the lonely beauty of such a woman might have been at peace.

"When you tried to seduce me," he said slowly, "I was required to resist. That did not mean that I found you unattractive, or that I was indifferent to your welfare, as I tried to advise you. Now that you have shown me what is within you, I ask you not to demean it by—this." He indicated the bottle, and discovered that he still held her hand.

This was an incidental intimacy more penetrating than all the dialogue and nakedness they had been practicing. She looked at him, realizing this, and gently disengaged herself. "A jug of gin," she said.

"I guess we got off on the wrong foot. I'm sorry." She did not touch the bottle.

The third picture was quite different. Savagery dominated it. A monster glared from a single eye, and behind it rose the head of an incredible snake, all teeth and no eyes or nose. Subble had never seen a combination so menacing.

"The omnivore of Nacre," Aquilon said.

The last painting showed the manta, immediately recognizable as the creature Veg had described. It was in full motion, probably as seen from the retreating tractor, and strangely beautiful.

"This is my mission," he said, studying it.

"I know." She laid her head on the table and cried.

Subble stood up and put the paintings away. He walked around the apartment and looked at the collected works, largely on mundane topics. Few of them had the magic of the four they had just looked at together. Aquilon had hinted that she disliked her present life, and her work proclaimed it. Her heart was on Nacre, with the two men she had known there and the creatures she remembered.

Behind him, she stirred, throwing away the bottle and going into the bathroom. He heard the water splashing wastefully, and knew she was trying to be sick.

He came across the pictures she had made of him: a spaceman staggering over a bleak moonscape, a handsome twentieth-century gentleman, an apeman swinging from a jungle tree, and a diver *au naturel*. Each likeness was accurate and detailed—and increasingly, from the first to the last, the special touch was there. The spaceman could have been anybody, but the diver was Subble. Not just an agent—Subble the individual. And, odd as it was to apply the thought to a picture of a naked man, Aquilon had put herself into it. She was astonishingly quick, for these were not mere sketches, and her skill was natural, not trained; her work really did reflect what was within her.

Subble was no artist, but interpretation of illustration was one of a number of things he was equipped to do with fair competence. He could learn a great deal about the character and mood of the artist by studying the technique.

He stood for some time contemplating the paintings.

His clothing still lay on the bed. He went to it.

Aquilon lay beside his suit, watching him. "You're giving up?"

He picked up his clothing, intending to take it to the other room before changing. "Two men already love you."

"And now you are modest," she said. "You don't want me to see your body again."

He walked to the door.

"Come here," she said.

He set his burden upon the chair beside the door and went to her.

Aquilon threw her arms about him and kissed him, drawing him down to lie beside her. "You know we can't make love now," she said.

"I know."

They lay embraced, the bathrobes decorously closed. "What happened to your invincibility?" she murmured in his ear.

"I saw what you are."

She nestled her head against his shoulder. "If only *I* knew what I am, I wouldn't be here."

"You are a truly beautiful woman. Your body has nothing to do with it."

His shoulder became damp from her tears. "Will you help me?"

"I will try."

"If only I *were* beautiful!" she exclaimed. "But I'm ugly in a way nobody can cure. If only I could choose, one way or the other. Veg and Cal are clean, in their ways, but I'm dirty, and I just can't choose which one to—to inflict myself upon. And now I've come between them, because I *can't* decide. And I can't even—"

She tensed and bit the hard muscles of his shoulder. "I can't tell you that. It's up to Cal. All I can do is—"

She paused, then rolled onto her back, closed her eyes, took his hand and told him about the omnivore.

* * *

Cal was breathing in pitiful gasps, but he spoke as soon as Veg was gone. "You shouldn't have done that, 'Quilon."

Aquilon plumped down beside him and delved into the pack. "He can handle that sort of thing much better alone," she said. "You and I would only be in the way." She unfolded a survival cup and drew out the container of water. "You'd better drink some of this."

"I don't think you understand," Cal said carefully, waving away the drink. "How well do you know Veg?"

She looked up in surprise. "Why, for three months, of course. Ever since I joined the expedition. We've gotten along well enough. But I thought you two were old friends."

"More than that," he said morosely. "We are a team: Brains and Brawn . . . and now Beauty, of course." Aquilon flushed gently. "Didn't you realize—"

Her flush paled all the way. "I forgot!" She scrambled lithely to her feet. "I'll go after him. I never meant to—"

"Please." Cal gestured her back tiredly. "He would never kill a harmless creature. He will decide it was a joke. Perhaps he will actually bring back a herbivore for you to admire. Perhaps it is just as well." He looked at the water she still held and turned away. "We can hardly have come three miles. I can't make it."

"Of course you can," Aquilon said. "I'll help you." But she was tired already. Twenty-one miles?

Cal shook his head regretfully and tried to smile. "It's not that, entirely. I could walk the distance, perhaps, with your help. But you see, I can't eat, either."

"You mean you're another—"

"No. It becomes . . . complicated . . . to explain. I can't eat off the land, as you might, and I have no supply of my own. I can't survive very long without it. The water might help, but I'll be dead long before we reach camp."

Aquilon opened her mouth but was unable to speak.

"Don't feel that way," Cal said softly. "I brought it on myself when I insisted upon coming along. It

84

was a calculated risk. I knew the moment the tractor failed that it was the end for me. The two of you will have a better chance if you don't wait for me to die."

"Cal—" She faltered. "I hardly know you as I thought I did, but—" She waved her hands in the air, characteristically trying to shape a concept that would not fit into words. "I just can't leave you here, no matter what. The omnivore—"

The little man shrugged. "I can only tell you that I have wanted to die for some time. Now fate has given me the opportunity. I'm not being sacrificial. For me, the end is clear—and I want to meet it alone."

Aquilon stared at him, feeling the pupils of her eyes contracting to black pits in the pallor of her face. She tried to control her physical reactions, but she had been hit too suddenly by too much. Cal's gaze did not falter. He was not an old man, but the narrow lines about his eyes and mouth tokened appalling suffering. No, he was not being sacrificial.

She set down the cup, knowing that he had refused to drink so that he would die more rapidly. "I'll go get Veg," she said, unable to face him longer.

"Strange," Cal said as he watched Aquilon work. "If this creature is a true carnivore—"

Aquilon did not look up from the carcass. Veg had dragged it to their "camp" and this surprising development had postponed discussion of Cal's fate for the time being. "We really can't tell, can we?" she asked. "We know the signals for Earth animals— the type of teeth, and so on—but this one doesn't have any teeth. I'm hoping that the lab experts will be able to tell from my pictures. But if it isn't like the herbivore or omnivore—"

"Call it a paleontologist's hunch," Cal said with animation. "This has the feel of a carnivore. The sleekness of it, the speed, the armament—look at the cutting edge of that tail!—this thing is organized to prey on the run. But what bothers me is, if it *is* our carnivore, why weren't the herbivores afraid of it? It must have been hiding right inside the herd."

"You know, he's right," Veg said, surprised. "You saw it first, 'Quilon. You say it came out of the bunch. But it just isn't natural for herbies not to be afraid of the hunter."

Aquilon looked up this time. "Herbies?"

"Well, what would you call them? You named the manta."

"All right," she said. "Herbies."

"Don't smile, now."

Aquilon didn't smile.

"Unless they knew it was impossible to get away," Cal mused. "Its speed is fantastic."

"But it only came out when we got there," Aquilon pointed out. "Why did it attack *us,* when the ... herbies ... were so much easier to catch?"

"It wanted to race again," Veg said. "Find out how it made out when we didn't have our machine along. Like a dog." He became sober, for had he believed that, he would not have surmounted his aversion to taking its life. "But we can't afford that kind of race, with it *or* the omnivore."

There was silence for a time. Mention of the omnivore had a tempering effect.

"This eye," Aquilon said. "I've never seen anything like it. It's almost as massive as the brain—and that brain is heavily convoluted."

"That, too, bothers me," Cal admitted. "I wish I could focus on the details, but without my glasses—"

Veg looked at the water container and put it aside regretfully. "Just how well do you figure it sees?"

"The eye is almost nine inches long and three in diameter," Aquilon said seriously. The sharp knife in her hand flashed as she aimed the spotlight at it and dexterously severed tissues. "There are so many major nerve trunks connecting it to the brain that it's almost impossible to tell where one leaves off and the other begins. The eye itself is filled with some sort of refractive fluid. It's almost like an electronic tube. There's no guessing its properties—but my estimate is that the manta can see a great deal better than we can."

"I agree," Cal said. His whole attitude was different when he had a problem to wrestle with. "This entire thing is an astonishing—"

"Barely an hour of daylight left, as I make it," Veg interrupted. "We have to move. We don't want to be caught in the open plain at night."

Cal frowned. "Veg, I want to tell you—"

" 'Quilon, you take the pack, if you can carry it; I'll handle Cal." Veg picked up the smaller man and hoisted him over his shoulders with careful strength. "We lost some time, here, but we can make it up if we move right along."

Aquilon silently rolled up her anatomical sketches, plunged the dissection knife into the ground to clean it, and struggled into the straps. Veg set the pace, a good four miles an hour, burden and all. Cal didn't try to speak again.

There was a single half-hearted trail up the side of the mountain ridge, twisting narrowly among the rainbow fungi and over the ledges and slopes. At the foot the fungus was brilliant—horns, spires, skyscrapers of it, layer upon layer like a candy fairyland; but two miles up only tired white blobs clung to the ledges, unable to take firm hold on the outcroppings of rock and unwilling to surrender the slim beachhead that they had. Even the dust seemed sparse and dry.

It was a tortuous ascent—yet something had made the trail, and something must use it still. And it led, generally, in the direction they were going.

They sat propped against the mountain at dusk, recovering from the exertion. Veg had not complained, but Cal looked bad and Aquilon hurt all over from the chafing weight of the pack. The air was cooler now, but this only seemed to intensify her thirst; no one would touch the quart of water.

Veg lifted one of the football fungi from its precarious perch. "You know, I kicked one of these, and my toe was wet."

Cal lifted his head. "Give me," he said.

Veg passed it over and the little man squeezed it experimentally. A few drops of fluid fell to the ground. "Let's look at this," he said.

Aquilon passed him a cup and he squeezed some more, letting the juice collect. "Here," Veg said. He took the fungus and pressed with both hands.

Liquid spurted between his fingers, filling the cup and overflowing onto his legs. "It's a water-sponge!" he exclaimed.

Cal held the brimming vessel and looked into its

depths. The fluid was almost transparent. He sniffed it. He put the cup to his lips.

"Hey!" Veg and Aquilon cried together.

"Water," Cal said complacently. "We have to be practical. If I survive it, we have a usable source. You two share the jug. By the time you need more, either you'll have it or your load will be lighter."

Aquilon looked at Veg and he looked at her. Cal was being practical, all right. He claimed to want to die, and without water he certainly would. He had nothing to lose from experimentation—and perhaps could gain a reprieve for them all.

They watched him drink down the cupful.

"I don't remember any mountain between us and the base," Aquilon said doubtfully. "Are you sure the compass—" She was fishing for a diversion from the morbid wait they were involved in.

"The compass is correct," Cal said, stretching out comfortably. "It works on the gyro-vector principle. This one was set at the base; as long as it runs, it has to be accurate."

Veg looked at the forbidding trail ahead. "I wish they'd made the distress signal on the gyro-victim principle, or whatever it is," he muttered. "Still almost twenty miles to go. Straight up and down, I figure."

That brought the conversation to a halt. The dusk was intensifying slowly, but little time remained for them to find a suitable location for the night.

"No time for talk," Veg said. "If we can find a good level ledge or somewhere safe, we'll be okay. 'Quilon, leave that pack there; I'll come back for it. But we'd better ditch anything we can spare. You take the rifle and some ammo—" He browsed through the pack, searching for things to remove. Soon there was a meager pile beside the fog-pistol. "No omnivores *here*," he said, seeing her glance at it.

She started to protest, but realized that she lacked the strength to haul either the pack or the surplus items farther. "You drink the water, then," she said.

He nodded, to her surprise, and upended the quart. She was sure he wasn't being selfish, though her thirst abruptly multiplied; he had something else in mind. Possibly he intended to conserve his strength to carry *her*, if Cal—

Veg was already on the move. She dropped the strap and followed him meekly up the mountain.

They climbed. Veg, indefatigable, carried his companion without seeming to lessen the pace at all, and Aquilon, packless as she was, strained to keep up. Night tightened about them; the mist seemed to take on a more physical substance and close in until little beyond the immediate trail was visible. The dust stirred up by their feet coated her body with grime. The path went on, rising to its hidden climax.

"Luck," Veg exclaimed. Aquilon, mistaking the word, caught up to him and looked ahead. They had come to an ideal ledge, hardly more than a widening of the path, but flat and almost level. The mountain sheered off so sharply above and below that it would be exceedingly difficult for any nocturnal prowler to approach them unaware.

Veg set Cal down. "Got to pick up that pack," he said to Aquilon, and disappeared into the night.

"Take the rifle!" she called after him. It was the one thing she had made certain not to leave behind, though even its slight weight had proved to be an enormous encumbrance at this pace. But he was gone, his quick heavy footsteps already muffled in the blank trail below.

Cal remained where he was, asleep or unconscious. Aquilon took off her blouse, afraid to think what his condition might mean, and rolled it up to place under his head so that he would not breathe the dust. She brought out her brush and sketching pad; these, too, she never forgot.

Cal opened his eyes a few minutes later to see her painting. "My God—where do you find the energy to paint?"

"Your god?" she replied, puzzled but thrilled to realize that he was better, not worse. Every moment that passed, now, was evidence that the sponge-fungus juice was safe to drink. "You have such quaint expressions."

He did not deign to reply, but watched her with a half-smile.

Aquilon faced the emptiness beyond the fungus-encrusted perimeter and stroked the brush across the surface of the canvasite. Color came once more in magical mechanism—but the mechanism stemmed from technology and the magic was her own. The brush was a compact, highly refined instrument, a sorcerer's wand in her practiced fingers. A touch on one of the concealed selection spots could produce and blend any combination of colors in the visible spectrum and feed it through the bristles in meager or generous flow. Veg had marveled that she could perform these shifts of hue and density so subtly, and she had told him that the brush was really an extension of her arm. That, said in jest, was close enough to the truth; she was no longer conscious of the control she exerted. She willed a shade of gray, it came; royal purple, it was there. The brush might as well have been programmed directly to her brain, or perhaps her soul, her creative being; the images she saw merged into a grand whole that reflected in the canvas.

People always asked her why she didn't use a camera. How could she explain to them the difference between a living brush and a dead machine? It was said that the artist distorted his image, while the camera was exact—but the truth was that the artist captured the living essence while the camera recorded one dead still-image, a mounted fragment of the animated series that was reality. In life there were no frozen scenes. If the lines of her brush were not as literal as those of the photograph, it was because the lines of *life* were less literal than those of death. By the time a living thing could be reduced to formula, it was no longer living.

But she had given up trying to explain this concept to people. Cal would comprehend it, and therefore he had never needed to ask. Veg had probably never thought about the matter; he accepted things as they were, and that too was good.

For the others—she murmured technical things, such as the fragility of good equipment and perishability of photographic emulsion; the distortion induced by alien radiation and wavelengths, the awkwardness of carrying heavy supplies and setting them up in emergency situations. "How could you make a color plate of an alien creature who appeared for only half a second unexpectedly, and never again?" she demanded. "But the brush is even slower!" the nameless arguer insisted. "Not for me." She meant that she could hold the image in her mind and paint it accurately before it faded, but they didn't understand.

No—the brush was compact and limitless, as the mind was limitless, and it would never be replaced by machine processing. Not on the frontier. Just as man would never be superseded by automation, where it counted. The machines and machine minds had tried to unravel Nacre—and the insidious molds and fungi had silenced them, while the explorer-colonists suffered and died.

"You match your painting," Cal said sincerely.

Aquilon turned away from him, overcome by an emotion she did not understand.

"I'm sorry," he said. "I didn't mean to hurt you. You and your work are elegant. No man could look upon either and not respond."

She put away her painting, but continued to look over the edge. There was nothing there to see; it was easy to believe that it was not a drop-off but a celestial curtain enclosing the ledge. There were no stars, of course. "Do you love me?" she asked, surprising herself.

"I'm afraid I do."

"That's really why you came—on the tractor."

He did not deny it.

She faced him again, knowing that her face was now no more than a pale blur shadowed by her hair. The fungi around the fringe of their little camp were luminescent, and soft pastels glowed in silent levels, red, yellow, blue and green. She wished she had realized this before she put away her painting; but probably the effect did not materialize until darkness was complete. The colors seemed bright, but were not; Cal was visible only as a darkness cutting off the decorations.

"Cal," she whispered, sounding like a frightened little girl. "Cal—would you love me if I were not beautiful?"

"I would love you."

She went to him, then, finding his hands in the dark and holding them in hers. "When I was six," she said, "I was pretty. Then the virus came. I was only sick for a day—but after that . . . I didn't even know. . . ."

"The sickness of our time," Cal murmured. " 'A terrible beauty is born.' "

"I—I thought I was *smiling,*" she said. "And they screamed. Every time I was happy, they beat me, and I didn't know why. I had to learn never to smile . . ." She caught her breath. "And they—they named me after the Northwest wind . . . the cold north wind. . . ."

He stroked her hair. "That was cruelty."

"They *knew,* while I was all confused. . . ."

" 'The best lack all conviction, while the worst are full of passionate intensity.' Forgive me, 'Quilon, for retreating to literature, but I cannot improve upon William Butler Yeats. There is too much sorrow in our existence."

"I don't *want* William Butler Yeats!" she flared. "I want *you!*"

"Yet you would change me," he reminded her gently.

She bowed her head so that the blonde hair obscured any of her face that might still be visible, still holding one of his hands. "We're different, you and I and Veg. We look . . . normal . . . but we're not.

We're torn and frightened and so very much alone.
. . ."

"That is a half-truth, 'Quilon. We—"

She laid her head on his shoulder, forgetful of his weakness. "I never realized that before. That there were others. We need each other, Cal, because we're only half-people by ourselves. You don't have the right to die, not by yourself, no matter what happened to you—"

Suddenly, surprisingly, she was sobbing. Cal put his arms around her, leaned back against the rock and the resilient molds upon it, and continued to stroke her fine hair. His manner showed that he had been touched, but remained resigned.

"I wish I could smile again. . . ." she said into his shoulder.

Aquilon woke when Veg's little spotlight played over them. Cal lolled against the rock; he had been too polite to ask her to move, and one of his hands still rested on her bare back. He too came awake, slowly.

"None of that now, friend," Veg said, not unkindly. "Put her down and come over here. We have a problem."

Aquilon sat up, lifted Cal's head and rearranged the wadded shirt so that he could face Veg without moving; but he elected to get up anyway. She shrugged and remained to put on her blouse. There seemed to be no doubt now: the fungus water was a success.

Veg set the pack down and flashed the light on it. "Do you see that?" he asked gravely.

"Somebody cut the straps!"

Veg laughed, a little hollowly. "Some*thing,* more likely," he corrected Cal. "Genuine surplus alligator-hide leather straps. Never liked 'em much myself, but you know *I* didn't do that. I had a terrible time toting that bundle all the way up here, and holding the beam too, to see the trail. Had to hold everything in my arms."

"But what could have—"

"Who else but Brother Manta?"

Aquilon considered, still on the far side of the shelf. "Yes, the manta could have done it. That means there're more than one in this area. But I really don't see why . . . and why just the straps?"

"It's just as well those creatures aren't equipped to climb very well," Cal said.

Veg took him by the shoulders and turned him around to face the trail below. Aquilon looked past them in the same direction.

There, less than twenty feet away, at the edge of the shelf, a single luminous eye was watching them.

Morning: the eye remained. They had slept, fitfully, under its awesome scrutiny. There was nothing else to do. Veg refused to fire at it, and they knew they could not escape it. This, she thought, might be the attitude of the herbivores: why flee or fight such a creature? Neither attempt could help.

By daylight there was certainty. It was the eye of another manta, perhaps the third they had seen, hunched near the end of their little plateau. Its stationary form was not so frightening, but knowing what they did of its nature they were hardly able to ignore it, either.

Aquilon got up, shaking off the inevitable film of

dust and stretching her limbs in a natural but dazzling manner. "I wish we'd saved the other one for food," she said. "I can mend the pack, but we still have to eat."

"We can try some of the white fungus," Veg said. "If the water's good, maybe the rest of it is too. That'll take care of us, at least until we get to the base."

"But even Earth mushrooms can kill you, and many of these are worse," Aquilon protested. "How can we take the chance?" She was hungry enough to do it, however.

"I tried some last night," Veg said, a little sheepishly. "Tasted terrible, but didn't hurt me. Better than the dust."

So he had followed Cal's example that quickly! "The dust?" she asked, shocked. "You tried eating—"

"The dust is organic," Cal said. "The sun never touches the surface of Nacre. That's why you don't see anything green, except as an occasional fungus decoration. But the living cells drift down steadily. Highly nutritious sediment, if you can stomach it, and the herbivores evidently have no trouble."

"Oh, I see," she said. "And the omnivores eat the herbivores . . . and so must our manta."

"The ecological pyramid," Cal agreed. "It has to exist. Of course the omnivores eat dust too, and fungus, or they'd be misnamed."

Veg carved a chunk from one of the more succulent footballs. "Whatever the manta is, it sure is fast on its foot. Probably has to be, to keep clear of the omnivore." He glanced at the animal, which sat unmoving at the edge. "Try this, 'Quilon, if you're hungry." He held out a chunk of the white substance.

She reached to take it.

The manta bounded into the air, its body assuming something like the dread racing shape. It hurtled between them.

Aquilon fell back with a cry. Veg stood frozen as the creature came to rest beside him, near the fungus. They stared at it.

"Are you *sure* it's tame?" Aquilon asked facetiously.

Veg watched it, baffled. "I thought I was done for, last night," he admitted. "When I saw that eye coming after me, and me without the rifle. But all it did was follow—that's when I began to be sorry about blasting that other. Maybe it *wasn't* attacking."

Cal spoke up from the far side. "I don't think it was attacking just now. It seemed to be trying to keep the two of you apart."

"Hands off the damsel?" Veg asked thoughtfully. "But last night the two of you were pretty close—"

Aquilon flushed. "Maybe it thought we were—"

"Now wait a minute," Veg exclaimed in mock anger. "A moralistic manta I can do without—at least, if it figures *me* as the extra man."

"Perhaps we should marry?" she murmured sweetly.

"I could never marry a—" Veg stopped, but it was there between them, a joke that hurt. She had mistaken his gallantry for genuine interest and he had set her straight. They were man and woman, but there was a fundamental difference in practice. She had thought his vegetarianism was only a personal preference, but now she saw that it affected his whole outlook on life.

By mutual consent they turned away from that subject, too.

"The fungus!" Aquilon said excitedly. "Maybe it *is* poisonous. Maybe it was trying to stop us from eating it!"

Veg still held the white mass. Slowly he brought it to his mouth, eying the creature beside him. The manta looked back, motionless. Veg took a bite.

Nothing happened.

"You try it," he said, tossing the remainder to Aquilon.

She caught it deftly and repeated the process as the manta swiveled smoothly to watch her. The faint putrescence of it made her gag. It was like eating rotten potato, but she forced her teeth to close on it. The manta did not respond. She looked at Cal, offering the morsel, but he shook his head negatively.

Veg shrugged. "I'll prepare a full, er, repast," he said, taking up the knife.

Aquilon went over to Cal. She knew he was hungry, and that for him a few hours of undernourishment were like starvation for a normal man. He simply did not have the physical resources to stand up under it. "What are you going to do?" she asked, looking into his eyes. "You told me you couldn't eat—"

"I don't suppose it would do any good just to tell you to leave me here and get on back to the main camp."

She shook her head no. "If you'll just tell us how we can help you—"

"You can't help me. I will die in a few hours, no matter what you do. If I could only convince you of the truth—"

Veg, slicing into more fungus, had been listening intently. "Maybe it's time you did tell us, Cal. I've known you for three years, and you never let out a word. You never come to the mess hall. What's the matter with you? Why are you always so weak you can hardly walk? Why can't you eat any of our food?"

Cal closed his eyes as if in pain. "You wouldn't understand."

Aquilon took his hands, as she had the night before. "We aren't going to let you die, Cal," she said. "We'll all stay here together."

Veg chewed on fungus, not disagreeing.

"Death is my destiny," Cal said, the words, from him, quite unmelodramatic. "Anything else I might tell you would be a lie."

"Then tell us the lie," Veg said around his mouthful.

Aquilon started, surprised by the simplicity of it. She kept forgetting that the big man's unsubtle mannerisms did not denote any obtusity of mind or feeling; he would not have been permitted in space were that the case. At one stroke he had nullified Cal's elaborate defensive structure.

Cal watched them both for some sign of relentment, but found none; Veg consumed his fungus entrée and Aquilon imitated him, more to keep up appearances than from present appetite. The stuff was foul.

"A story, then," Cal said at last. "Then you go on—the two of you."

There was no response.

"I was only a paleozoologist searching for fossils," Cal said, closing his eyes. "You can't generally locate a given specimen just by digging a hole in the ground. My specialty was Eocene insectivores and I was running down a rumor that a primitive primate shinbone had been spotted in a sedimentary outcrop. It happened to be in a restive corner of the world, and I hadn't paid sufficient attention to local politics. I didn't even speak the language."

"I don't believe a word," Veg said equably.

"I was arrested as a spy—that was one word I picked up in a hurry!—and was unable to convey the true nature of my mission to them. My captors didn't understand paleontology; I think their religion renounced any nonbeatific derivation of man. They were convinced I was concealing information, and they had devious methods of coercion. They were not backward in the *modern* biological sciences. Odd how retrogression and advancement sometimes coexist. . . ." He trailed off.

"What did they do to you, Cal?" Veg inquired. "According to your story, I mean."

Cal went on with a visible effort. Aquilon was shocked to see the fatigue and misery of years so deeply etched upon his face. "It doesn't matter now, except for one thing. My diet became . . . restricted. They fixed it so that I can't live on anything but—" He stopped.

"We have to know," Aquilon said softly.

". . . blood."

There was silence for several minutes.

Veg walked over to the pack at last and withdrew a cup. He squatted down. "Can you take it straight," he asked, abandoning pretense, "or does it have to be by transfusion?"

Cal's self-control dissolved, embarrassing Aquilon acutely. What had happened to the intellectual power she had so admired in Cal? This was a moaning baby of a man. Would it have been kinder to let him die?

"They made me into a vampire," Cal whispered. "I've been living on plasma ... have to go to the doctor for my meals. He's the only one on the ship that knows. The grouping—RH factor—doesn't matter; I take it orally. How I've wanted to die!"

Aquilon whirled as the meaning of Veg's question sank in. "You can't—" she cried.

Veg was carefully sterilizing his knife in the flame of one of the matches. "Keep out of this," he said gruffly.

He must have known. He had taken the last of the water so that he would have ... blood. "But you can't even kill a herbivore," she said, distracted. "How can you—"

Veg wiped off his arm and readied the knife. Aquilon made as if to throw herself upon him, then subdued herself.

She had thought she understood the motivations of these men, and thought they understood each other—but her knowledge of anatomy, human and animal, and her associated studies left her convinced that Cal's story *was* a lie. No drug or surgical technique she knew of could possibly do to a man what Cal claimed; the nearest approach would be regression to an infantile dependence on milk, which was in fact very similar to blood. But if it *could* be limited specifically to blood, yet not so narrowly as to restrict the condition of that blood or the animals from which it came, a chemically similar substitute could certainly be prepared in the laboratory in quantity. The oral dosage was the giveaway—a transfusion was a precise business, but the digestive tract of man was equipped to handle a variety of things.

Cal had indeed made up a story, as he had threatened—and Veg must have recognized it for what it was. Why, then, was Veg accepting the fiction as fact—*and acting upon it?* How could he donate, literally, his own blood, for the perpetuation of a charade?

And then she understood.

"I don't think I ever knew what real friendship ... was," she said quietly. "But you have to save your strength to carry him. Otherwise we won't get back at all, any of us."

Veg hesitated. "He's got to eat."

She held out her own arm. "I don't have to carry anything," she said.

Veg studied her and nodded. "You're pretty much of a woman," he said, and there was a double meaning there, as there had to be. It erased his prior reaction to the bantering suggestion of marriage, and the motive behind it.

He lurched to his feet and charged past her.

Turning, she saw the reason. Cal had almost made it to the edge. There could be no doubt about his intent. Veg caught the little man and carried him back to the inner side.

"You don't know what you're doing," Cal gasped weakly. "I *need* to die—"

"You don't have a choice," Veg said. "Unless you

want to spill *her* blood into the dust." He returned to Aquilon, carrying the knife.

Once again the manta moved, flashing between them with alarming speed.

"What the—" Veg grunted, angry now. "You can touch Cal; I can touch Cal. But it won't let me touch you. What's the matter with the critter?"

"Throw me the knife," Aquilon said.

Gritting her teeth against the pain and shock, she made a neat surgical slice across the fleshy part of her forearm and let the rich blood drip into the cup.

The four moved on up the slope. Veg led the way, carrying Cal on his shoulders; Aquilon followed, bearing the rifle and her sketch-pad; last came the manta, hopping erratically. It evidently wasn't accustomed to slow travel. Aquilon remained nervously aware of it, almost feeling the slash of the tail down her exposed back, but it never came too close.

The sheer side of the mountain began to level out, as they neared what had to be the top of a convex slope. The spherical fungi became larger and more numerous, lining the trail like fat snowmen, and the candyland smaller growths reappeared.

The ground shuddered. Loud crashing and pounding approached from the obscurity above. Something was charging down the trail! Veg lowered Cal to the side and whirled. "Only one thing makes a noise like that," he said grimly.

Aquilon gripped the rifle and pressed the ignition stud, feeling the warmth of the chamber in her hands. It occurred to her now, as she saw the jet of water vaporize inside the translucent barrel, that they could have distilled the fungus-water, cooking out the bacteria and eliminating the poisons that might have been in solution.

The rifle was hot and ready to fire. Veg strode toward her, reaching for the weapon. The manta leaped and flared ominously. He backed away. "Throw it here!"

Too late. A great mottled shape came hurtling out of the mist ahead. It would weigh, Aquilon knew, in the neighborhood of a thousand pounds. Its spiny, discolored skin hung in huge folds, making the creature resemble an enormous horned toad. A single tiny eye was embedded in the flesh of its forepart, glaring balefully out. This was animosity incarnate. This was the omnivore.

Cal, nearest to it, huddled on the ground. The savage beast leaped, too anxious for its prey, and the great blotched shape passed over him, the sharp teeth of its striking tail clashing together just inches from his head.

Aquilon was before the monster now, the rifle hissing in her hands. The omnivore turned on her, raising its stout tail overhead. The vicious jaws in it gaped as that tail wove from side to side like a deadly serpent, doubly dangerous because it was a most specialized weapon of offense. There was no connecting alimentary tract, no soft tissue, no weak spot. Those jaws could crunch a human arm in half, and the tail could hurl a human body into the air and dash it against a rock or under the slavering underside.

Her bullets only stung it, and she had no time to put a shell in the other chamber. The massive propulsive muscles of the omnivore's single foot bunched, ready for the next leap.

Veg stepped in from the side, shouting, trying to distract the omnivore's attention, though he was armed only with the puny knife. The monster swiveled, aware of him in spite of the foolish cries; it could not, of course, hear him, but its perceptions were more diversified than those of other Nacre creatures, and it could smell him and feel the warmth of his body. The jaws of its tail clashed together loudly as it turned on this new adversary.

The manta, temporarily quiescent, came back to life. It rose into the air, once more assuming the shape that had earned it its name. The eye seemed to flash as the creature banked around both humans and landed before the omnivore.

Facing the monster, the manta was tiny. Four feet tall when stationary, it could not have weighed more than eighty or ninety pounds, Earth-gravity. Yet the bulking omnivore recoiled; it leaped back, turning in the air. Its toothed tail came back as a kind of rear guard, intersecting the second jump of the manta.

The disk of the manta spread out, suddenly huge. Aquilon could feel the wash of air as it took off. It passed over the omnivore. There was a sharp Crack! as of the snap of a whip—and the gruesome jaws at the tip of the monster's tail were flying through the air directly at Veg. He jerked back—and toppled over the edge of the path.

With a cry, Aquilon rushed to the brink, light-headed from the exertion and the loss of the blood she had donated. Veg was rolling helplessly down the side, puffball fungi shattering and squirting under him but cushioning his descent. He careened into one of the giants, bounced off as though it were a rubber boulder, and fetched up with his head buried in a smaller growth.

Aquilon scrambled down to help him, glad that the slope was less ferocious here than it had been lower on the mountain. As she got there, panting and dizzy, Veg straightened and spat white chunks out of his mouth.

"Are you all right?" she asked foolishly.

"Gimme a little—phew!—kiss and we'll find out," he replied, smiling. It was more fungus he was clearing out, not an insult to her.

Overcome by relief, she returned the smile.

She saw him blink, then tighten his jaw muscles in a spastic effort at facial control. Horror showed in the narrowing of his eyes.

Behind him the shape of the manta appeared, sailing down the steep slope. Its eye centered on Aquilon. Suddenly the body folded and swerved in a tangible double-take.

Too late she realized what she had done. Veg had seen. She had appalled him with her smile, that shameful thing she had tried never to show again. Now anything that might have built between them was gone. She knew what it was to wish for immediate death. Death ...

"Cal!" she cried, remembering. "He's still up there with the—"

Veg launched himself up the slope, followed lopingly by the manta. Aquilon started after them, but her head began to spin again almost immediately. She had exerted herself too much already, and there had been the shock of the ... smile. But life went on, and there were other things to worry about. She eased her pace and picked her way up carefully.

She reached the trail, afraid for what she might see. There had been no sound from Veg—or anything else. It was too quiet.

The omnivore lay dead, its body slashed into tattered sections as though a cosmic knife had dropped upon it. Pale blood dripped from the carcass, forming rivulets across the flesh and soaking into the dust beneath, as thick and slow as that of a man. Cal was trying to gather some of it in his cup.

It was a horrible sight, ludicrous and pitiful at once. Somehow the notion that Cal should try to drink the blood of the omnivore disturbed Aquilon even more than had the donation of her own. Yet it was the obvious solution, if they were to survive at all as a group; her present disorientation proved that her resources in this respect were severely limited. The wrenching of it suppressed the shock of the other thing, the smile, for the moment.

It was right. It was a stroke of fortune. The omnivore could feed them, and the risk the consumption of its flesh and blood entailed was no greater than the one they had already taken eating the loathsome fungus or drinking its juice. If it worked, it spelled life for all of them, instead of a cruel death.

It was still sickening.

Something nudged her foot, making her jump and look down. The jaws of the omnivore's tail were lying there, like the head of a mutilated dog, snapping reflexively with a lingering life of their own.

Muscle fibers trailed from the stub, tangling with the dust in clotted strings.

Aquilon leaned over the edge and gave way to silent nausea.

III. A Book of Verses

CAL'S HOUSE FRONTED the flexing water of the Gulf of Mexico. Subble had looked in vain for a private landing spot in the intensely developed suncoast of Florida, and had finally had to settle on the water, to the distress of the water-skiers ranging there. He anchored his flyer to the shallow bottom-land, allowed for the change of tide, and swam to shore.

Cal was working in the sun just beyond the seawall. He was small, standing a little over five feet, and not well-fleshed, but his skin was tanned and his movements sure. He gave no sign of any unusual weakness.

Before him, or rather around him, was an electronic device comprised of massed wires, a television chassis, ham radio equipment and laboratory mechanisms ranging from a pencil-soldering iron to a sophisticated pocket oscilloscope.

"Good," Cal remarked as Subble swam to the wall and heaved himself onto the pavement. "I need extra hands at this point."

"Aquilon called you," Subble said, shaking off the salt water.

"And Veg. Those two try to look out for my

welfare, as I think you know. I owe them a great deal."

Subble nodded, remembering the bloodletting episode Aquilon had described. He also understood by the man's entire attitude and immediate reactions that Cal was by far the most formidable of the persons on his list, physical evidence to the contrary. The man was extremely intelligent, and evidently approached the interview with a clinical rather than defensive manner. There was no bluster in him and no overconfidence; Subble was a situation to be explored and a hypothesis to be verified. Cal would ascertain the facts and let the consensus be his guide. Yet he was concealing something important, just as the others had done.

"I think we understand the situation," Cal said. "And this equipment should be no mystery to you."

"A jury-rigged closed-circuit television transceiver adapted to the signal emitted by the manta's eye," Subble said.

"Yes. We were slow to comprehend the nature of the creature. We assumed that it saw in much the way we do, though 'Quilon's dissection refuted that. But of course ordinary optics would be ineffective on a hazy world like Nacre. Just as the fish of the sublevels of the ocean become luminous—"

Subble was studying the schematics. "This is highly adaptible."

"Highly imprecise, you mean. I am not an electrical engineer, and until this is tested in the field it must be generalized. And testing is a problem."

"I saw the manta in the forest with Veg, and I smelled another in Aquilon's basement," Subble said quietly. "I presume the first fed on wildlife and the second on rats. At least two other mantas have been at this spot within the past two days, and your equipment has been in operation. Why is testing a problem?"

Cal was not alarmed. "Importation of unregistered aliens is illegal, for one thing. We called them pets, but that was a misnomer, and your presence here indicates that the government is getting suspicious. These creatures are dangerous, for another thing. Even you, with all your strength and skill, would be virtually helpless against a single manta."

Subble did not comment. He explored a large fibrous container, noting the pockets and fastenings inside. It was designed to hold the assembled transceiver, and to float on water. He glanced out over the gulf.

"Yes, they can 'walk' on water," Cal said. "At high speed the water presents a surface as solid as the dust nature trained them for. But the air here is thin, for them."

"When will I meet them?"

Cal shook his head. "I know you have no fear of death—but a premature encounter would be disastrous, for you and perhaps for Earth."

"Not for the manta?"

Cal tried to lift an energizer pack into the basket, but his strength was insufficient. Subble took it from him and fastened it in the proper place. Obviously the little man had not intended to take this equipment out to sea by himself.

"We live in a charged environment," Cal observed. "So many billions of sentient individuals, such intense war hysteria, cultural unrest, pressure to succeed. Most of the people of this planet are des-

perate to get away from it all—but there is nowhere
to go. Only a few qualify for space. And so they
grasp at anything in reach, and pull it down in the
belief they are climbing—"

Subble remembered the misery of the programmer
in charge of the cellar farm, and Aquilon's own
distraught emotionalism. He quoted:

The Sensual and the Dark rebel in vain
Slaves by their own compulsion. In mad game
They burst their manacles and wear the name
Of Freedom, graven on a heavier chain!

"Coleridge," Cal agreed. "He referred to the
French Revolution, of course, two hundred years
ago, but he spoke for humanity as well, as the great
poets do. 'When France in wrath her giant limbs
upreared'—how easy it would be to transpose that
for today!"

Subble smiled. "When Man in wrath his nuclear
arms upreared, And with that oath which smote air
earth and sea Fired his great jets and swore he would
be free—Bear witness how I hoped and feared!"

"Except that some of us no longer hope. Man is
an omnivore, figuratively as well as literally. He
consumes. everything—"

"An omnivore," Subble murmured, remembering
Aquilon's remarks.

"You begin to see the problem. Man is the true
omnivore, far more savage than the creature we
designated by that term on Nacre. I'm afraid it hit
'Quilon pretty hard when she realized—"

"It did. She won't touch meat now."

'I know exactly how she feels. Nacre was a pretty

drastic lesson. But none of us realized the really fundamental difference between man's nature and that of the creatures of Nacre. As it was, we were casting about blindly."

"So am I," Subble hinted. "What is this 'fundamental' difference, if it is not the ecological adjustment or the methods of perception?"

"I can't make that clear unless I tell you first about the third kingdom."

"I don't follow you." This sounded like a fairy tale, but the man had something concrete in mind.

Cal nodded. "Probably you overlook it just as we did on Nacre. I certainly had little excuse. All the learning in the world can't make a man grasp the obvious, when that learning contributes to a prescribed mode of thinking. This, more than the sensory differences, makes it difficult to establish full contact with the manta."

Subble studied him, but found no evidence of equivocation. The man had a concept that was not easy to accept or discuss, particularly for him, and the odds were good that it had direct bearing on what Veg and Aquilon had not felt free to tell him. There was a major section of the puzzle missing. "What must I do to acquire this information?"

"It is not information per se; it is a way of thinking. I haven't mastered it myself, and may never do so, though I like to think I am gaining ground. But it is a difficult route, especially for someone like yourself. You have too much contemporary power."

"Too *much?*"

"That can be a liability. There are realms only the impoverished can achieve."

Subble smiled again. "And again I say unto you,

it is easier for a camel to go through the eye of a needle, than for a rich man to enter the kingdom of God."

"I'm afraid that's what I mean. You have chosen one of the most popular misquotes of the language, and are probably not even aware of it."

"I assure you the quote is exact. King James Version, Matthew XIX:24."

"Precisely. You have been indoctrinated with a standard education, and a remarkably comprehensive one. You therefore have not reaped the benefits of genuine scholarship. You are limited by the standard restrictions and errors. I daresay you can quote the entire Bible—"

"I can."

"Yet you have never thought to question the version or translation. Otherwise you would have suspected that Jesus of Nazareth, in whatever capacity He existed, probably never spoke of a camel attempting anything so ludicrous as climbing through the eye of a needle. I believe the original term was 'rope,' or 'camel-hair,' miscopied and never corrected."

Subble was silent. It was true: he had no means to verify or refute this statement, but it had the ring of authenticity. It made no difference whether the little man was right or wrong; he had the advantage because his knowledge was more pertinent than Subble's own. Cal had pinpointed the weakness of a man who had his entire education grafted on, and Cal was in control.

For the time being. Well, Aquilon had warned him.

"The information doesn't matter," Cal said. "It is

the *attitude* that counts. You were sure of yourself because you knew you had your quotation straight. You were right, yet wrong. That's why your rich man has so much difficulty—he can't bring himself to part with his wealth, even when it becomes an impediment to the achievement of his basic desires. The poor man has no moral advantage; he simply has less to lose. So he can travel where the rich man can't."

"You are telling me that I must give up my knowledge if I am to complete my mission?"

"Essentially, yes. At least you must set aside your confidence in it. Your certainty will betray you, here."

"Can you provide me some more tangible reason for doing so?"

"That sounds like my cue to condemn you as a materialist who will never achieve the kingdom of heaven! But I don't require blind faith in anything, including faith itself. I can give you reason: you must learn to communicate with the manta, and the manta is alien. Much more alien than its actions or appearance indicate. Perhaps in time normal man will hold meaningful dialogue with normal manta—but not for many years, I suspect. You need to do it *now*— and that means you must go to the manta. You have to meet it on its own territory, in its own framework. No human conventions will help you; they'll only interfere. You may never get a second chance, if you blunder early."

Again Subble remembered Aquilon's episode, and knew that what Cal said was true. The manta's appearance was strange and its actions stranger— and the reactions of the three who had dealt with it on its home world were stranger yet. If he were to learn the whole truth, he would have to finish with the mysterious manta—and it obviously was alien. He could not trust the second-handed impressions of others.

But if he set aside his formidable training, he would be vulnerable—as perhaps the starfaring trio had been. Assuming that he *could* set it aside. "Do you realize what kind of conditioning I have undergone?" Subble inquired. "No casuistry can shake my logic; no torture can break me; no brainwashing can overcome my loyalty to my mission without first killing me. How do you propose that I accomplish what my entire existence was conceived and shaped to prevent?"

"I'm not sure, but I believe you can approach the third kingdom—and with that and my equipment you have a chance. The trick is to lead you there without destroying your mind. Trust me and let me guide you as far as I can and—we'll see."

"Why should I trust you?"

It was Cal's turn to smile. "Because I am completely sincere. You can read my emotion easily, and I know it and you know I know. You must believe me—or renounce faith in your own abilities, which is the same thing. So you have no choice."

Mousetrapped again, this time by paradox. His abilities *did* inform him that he had to question them. "This statement is false," he said, musing at it. Taken alone, those four words negated themselves, and forced a new framework which excluded them. An intellectual toy—but it had come to life. "All right. Lay on, Macduff. Lead the way to the third kingdom. I follow."

"And damn'd be he that first cries 'Hold, enough!'" Cal said. He went inside and returned with an ornate copper vessel resembling an antique teakettle, but slung lower. He set it on the pavement and touched a lighter to its spout. After several attempts he got it going with a tiny greenish flame perched just beyond the projecting tip.

"A lamp," Subble observed. "Aladdin's lamp?"

"Something like it. It generally takes a little while for Myco to appear, however. We'll talk; you tell me when you see him."

"Myco—a combining form applying to fungus. An unflattering designation."

"Not necessarily." Cal indicated a spot beside the lamp and they took their places crosslegged on the tile.

Subtle perfume wafted from the flame: cedar and more obscure aromas blended in a harmony new to him. He ticked the ingredients off in his mind, classifying each automatically, but there was a residue that escaped him. An unusual incense, certainly, but harmless. Evidently Cal was trying to create a mood for whatever he was leading up to.

"You have met Veg and 'Quilon already," Cal said, "and you know something of the situation we found ourselves in on Nacre. You know about the omnivore?"

"Yes."

"I suppose it seems a striking coincidence that our particular trio happened to possess the very qualities necessary for survival there."

"Yes. My boss views such coincidences with distrust. There is generally more to them than what is visible on the surface—or in the official reports."

Subble stared at the flame, waiting for the trap to spring. He detected no aliens nearby, but Cal was expecting something momentarily.

"Actually, there was no coincidence at all," Cal said. "Our unusual qualities were at best incidental to the problem, and contributed to some confusion. We just happened to be the group that became isolated on Nacre at the time contact was scheduled to be made. Anyone could have done it."

That was not precisely true. Cal had hold of information which frightened him thoroughly, and his bodily processes reflected it on every level. Veg and Aquilon had suspected, but Cal *knew*—whatever it was.

"Chance threw us together, but it meant nothing," Cal said. "I wish it would throw us together again."

"Triangle and all?"

"Triangle and all. 'Quilon has this thing about choosing, when really it isn't necessary. Love is not exclusive."

"She said she felt 'unclean.' "

Cal sighed. "The sensual and the dark rebel in vain," he said. His form was hazy through the gathering smoke of the lamp. "Slaves by their own compulsion. Earth has become a population of neurotics, turning inward what they can no longer dissipate outward. Acquaint yourself with virtually any person living today and you will discover it. Suppressed madness. That much certainly is not coincidence. No unique qualities remain—only unique ways to express the horror of continued existence. Some call it creativity, others psychoneurosis—but it remains the madness of a people who has lost its last rational frontier."

"Veg—"

"Convinced himself that death was the evil he had to fight. Fortunately, he was satisfied to restrict it to the refusal to kill unnecessarily, or to consume the flesh of any creature with a tangible instinct of self-preservation. He was never deeply touched, and remains one of the best adjusted members of our society. He's happy—while his forest lasts."

Subble had his doubts about that, but was trying to follow Cal, not debate with him. "Aquilon—"

"Was hit by it in childhood. She was a pretty girl, envied for her appearance. Some chance occurrence suggested to her that she should punish herself by sacrificing her smile. That way the others would not resent her. She took the injunction too literally, and the retribution was far more savage than the offense. Oh, yes, she was beaten—but that was the ignorance of her family, who took the symptom for willful meanness, though she was actually a rather wonderful person underneath."

"Yes," Subble said, remembering. "But she smiles now."

"And she's worse off than before. She's caught in a more devious complex. When she believed that the destruction of her smile exonerated her, she was free of other phobias and compulsions. Now she searches for them. She's trying to follow Veg's path, as though death were the ultimate evil—and of course it isn't. *Life* is our world's problem. Too much human life on Earth, crowding in so tightly that territory and freedom are largely concepts of the past. Death is the greatest privilege granted to man; death is responsible for his very evolution. Death is not our enemy—it is our salvation."

121

"That's an unusual view in itself." The perfumed smoke was exhilarating.

"It is the paleontologist's view. Anyone who studies the history of life on Earth must come to respect death as a vital force. Without death there would be no natural selection; without selection, chordate, mammal and man would never have arisen. The weak, the deviant, the outmoded—these must all make room for progress. Species radiation and selection: constant variations, some good, most bad, but on the whole the good ones survive and propagate. When you interfere with the selective process, you destroy man."

"And we have interfered," Subble said, seeing the reasoning but not the point of it. Cal was still working up to it. "We have preserved *every* human life, strong and weak, and nature cannot act."

"Oh, nature can act—but not in what we consider to be normal fashion," Cal corrected him. "I think our genie is on his way. Do you see him?"

Subble peered at the flame. He had been about to inquire about the nature of Cal's own malady, but had missed his chance. Or perhaps he had been outmaneuvered again. "Myco of the third kingdom? I'm afraid not."

"There above the lamp—like a little whirlwind, growing. Gray, at first, becoming lighter as it expands. Stop trying to be reasonable and *look*."

"If you insist." Subble concentrated—and saw it. The green flame flickered, changing color, gold, purple and bright red, and from the spout emerged a fine column of smoke, gray and whirling swiftly. As he watched it increased, a dust-devil, a miniature tornado, a burgeoning dervish, suddenly exploding into a giant dusky man garbed in streamers of thick smoke. "I see it," he said.

The genie placed clublike hands on hips and stared at him.

"Good," Cal said. "Myco will guide us to the third kingdom."

Subble jumped up, realizing that he'd been had again. "Psychedelic drug! Lysergic acid diethyla- mide—"

The genie laughed, and the sound echoed. The back of his head resembled a colored toadstool, and his teeth were tusks.

"LSD? No," Cal said. "This is a hallucinatory agent, though both are derived originally from mushrooms. Their properties differ in ways that wouldn't be important to you."

"This is the basis of your new philosophy?" Sub- ble inquired, disappointed. He reached to snuff out the lamp.

"No. It is merely a vehicle, a channel—that may or may not lead to the contact we seek. Give it a fair trial before you turn away."

"There is nothing in my mind not already avail- able to me," Subble said, but he let the flame be. "No mysteries can be unveiled where none exist. But the distortion induced by the drug can prejudice my effectiveness."

"Your mind is still closed. Look at yourself: are you elated? Depressed? Do you feel as though you are floating? Have your horizons become limitless? Are you nearer to God? Sexually precocious? Just what effect has the drug had upon your system? How has it incapacitated you?"

Subble ran through a quick series of physical and

intellectual exercises. "It has affected my system very slightly," he admitted. "Not enough to interfere with my performance significantly."

"In what way has it changed you, then?"

Subble looked at the standing genie, who stared contemptuously back at him. "It has provoked a sustained hallucination."

The genie bellowed. "O fool of a mortal—and I breathed upon thee one tiny breath, thou would fly into the sea and drown most foully, nor could thou do aught contrary!"

"Don't provoke Myco," Cal warned. "In the physical world, you may be supreme—but this is not your world. It does not follow your rules."

"Yeah," Myco said with satisfaction.

"Whose rules does it follow?" Subble inquired, interested.

"Mine," the little man said. "This drug produces hallucinations without inhibiting the conscious mind or affecting the thinking processes, except to the extent the hallucinations themselves affect them. You are in complete control of your mind and body—but I control the habitat."

"A shared dream?"

"Call it that for convenience. Actually, your view is built up from discreet hints I provide—key words and the use of the lamp which you could not fail to associate with Aladdin's escapade—but what you see naturally differs somewhat from what I see, as our knowledge and tastes vary. When it comes down to it, this is a fact of life anyway; one person can never be certain, for example, that the color he sees as red is not blue to his neighbor: the blue his neighbor calls red. In this respect the change is not great, and perhaps the drug really produces a closer accord, since any honest difference can quickly be reconciled, when challenged, with the dominant view. The weaker will conforms to the stronger will."

"How can you be certain that your will is stronger than mine?"

"Do you want tangible proof or a reasoned explanation?"

"Both."

"Is Myco wearing a turban?"

"No—his head is blatantly bare."

"Look again."

"He is wearing a turban."

"You are mistaken."

The genie was bareheaded again. Subble concentrated, trying to visualize the turban that had appeared for a moment, but nothing changed. Myco grinned at him, enjoying it. "It appears the genie obeys his master," Subble admitted.

"Yes. First, he is *my* image, a figment of *my* selection, well rehearsed by me, while you are meeting him for the first time. I probably know much more about Arabic mythology than you do, and that gives me power, just as my attitude toward the Bible translation gave me the advantage there. Now the situation is clearer, thanks to the literal nature of the drug's imagery. You could not control Myco unless you knew more about him."

"Yeah," Myco repeated.

"Second, I have been here many times before— under the drug, I mean—and I have developed tolerance and control. I am under less deeply than you are, though we have taken the same dose, and that gives me a firmer grip on objectivity as we both know it. Experience is the best teacher, particularly here."

Subble studied the genie, intrigued by the creature's evident reality despite agreement that he was a product of the imagination. Realization that a fear was groundless was supposed to banish it—but he knew it often did not. Knowledge that an illness was psychosomatic did not always ease the pain, either. Suddenly he sympathized with a host of problems he would ordinarily have observed dispassionately—the problems of desperate individuals on a crowded world. He *knew* the genie did not exist—but this didn't change a thing. There it stood, as the unfounded fears and problems stood before others.

"I can read thy mind, too," Myco said. "Not that it pleasureth me."

"Finally, your own preference betrays you," Cal said. "You do not *want* to take control, because that would abort your mission. You don't need supremacy, you need information—and you know that I can only give it to you this way."

"I do not remember past experiences, of course," Subble said, "but I suspect that you and Veg and Aquilon represent the damnedest trio I have encountered. I'd certainly like to see the interplay between you when you three are together."

Cal smiled a little sadly. "It is a quartet now: physique, emotion, intellect—and spirit. Perhaps, soon, we *shall* be together again. We cannot endure apart."

Subble perceived that the little man was not thinking of the romantic aspects. There was something else, just as there had been for the others. Cal had been correct: every person on Earth was pressured into an odd configuration, but these three had a peculiar interaction that gave them something special.

"But we have other business," Cal said briskly. "Myco, show the vault."

"I hear and obey!" the genie boomed. He stooped and touched the floor. A great silver ring appeared, arabesqued inside and out, and screwed vertically into the center tile. Myco hauled on this and the slab came up to reveal a staircase going down.

"Down there?" Subble inquired, no longer bothering to distinguish between types of reality. "Not the black hole of Calcutta?"

"Another fallacy," Cal said. "That episode is entirely fictional. It was a rumor which even historians took as fact, since it seemed to justify British policy in India."

"I see. But in *this* edition your genie could shut us in securely and take over the hallucination."

"An interesting thought," Cal said. "But a chance we'll have to take. You have to experience the marvels of the third kingdom, to appreciate them properly. This is important."

"As you say," Subble agreed. His remark had not been serious, but now he wondered.

Myco shrank somewhat in size, manifested a torch, touched it to the flame of the lamp and held it there until it caught. He led the way into the ground.

The stairs descended into a vaulted corridor lined with heavy closed doors. "The third kingdom is rich in all the needs and comforts of man," Cal said. "Here is the chamber of food. Observe it well." The genie opened the door with a flourish and stood beside it at attention as the two men entered.

It was a gourmet's delight. An enormous banquet table had been set up, groaning with exotic delicacies. An entire stuffed pig squatted in a platter at the head place, garnished with fragrant herbs and spices and relishes. Beyond it was a monstrous roast turkey nestling in matted parsley, and beyond that a line of salmon steaks decorated with stewed raisins and sliced lemon.

They walked down the interminable length of it, past creole shrimp, meat loaf and lamb shish kebab. There were towering salads—chicken, tuna, potato, gelatin and fruit, with dressings too numerous and exotic to number. There were steaming tureens of soup and aromatic breadstuffs and pastries. There was chocolate cake and strawberry pie. Fresh corn on the cob steamed beside golden carrots and thick pods of okra ... jelly omelet ... potato pancakes. Table wines of every description stood adjacent to their traditional dishes, and after them were boiling coffee and frosty ice cream.

Agents sometimes found themselves in odd situations, in the line of duty.

They completed the gustful circuit and returned to the hall. "Impressive?" Cal inquired, and again there was a subtle extra meaning there.

"Impressive. Can any of it be eaten?"

"Oh, yes, and most enjoyably. But you would be hungry again the moment the vision ended. That's the trouble with magic—no residual effect."

"Suppose there were actually more commonplace food available?"

"You could feast on it delightfully, and afterwards you would have a full stomach and a pleasant memory."

Subble appreciated how easily a craze could form.

Myco had not bothered to accompany them inside. He stood at the door holding his nose.

"Our next display is within the chamber of health," Cal said, gesturing. The door opened.

The room was large—so large it seemed they were emerging into a valley. Just ahead was an open plain bounded by vigorous trees: beech, ash, maple and a solitary bull spruce. Bronzed Greek athletes were taking exercise: one throwing the javelin, another heaving the discus, four indulging in a foot race and two wrestling strenuously. Down the valley two vibrant young women in shorts were playing tennis. The men looked like Veg, the women like Aquilon. A man resembling Subble himself was practicing elaborate dives into a rippling pool, naked.

The air was bracing, with a crisp occasional breeze. The grass underfoot sprang up luxuriantly, and nothing showed, animal or vegetable, that was not in the prime of life.

"And wealth," Cal said, leading the way to the third chamber. Myco had disappeared.

It was a palace comprising many chambers in itself. The first was filled with gold and silver coins of rare and handsome design, some round, some hexagonal, some holed in the center, overflowing from great jars and piled haphazardly upon the floor. Subble estimated the weight of metal and calculated its net value in modern terms: over eleven million dollars for what was visible in this room alone, discounting the antique or archaeological enhancement of the strange old coins.

The second room was more impressive: jewels of every color and description—blue diamonds, green emeralds, red rubies, star sapphires and assorted lesser gems, some splendidly faceted, others gleaming in natural crystalline formations. There were strings of pearls and intricate rings and bracelets.

The third room held priceless paintings and statuary: Subble recognized the handiwork of Michelangelo, Da Vinci, van Gogh, Picasso and many other masters, all represented by originals. A number he did not recognize, except by type: Chinese Ming, Maya Jaina, Egyptian Middle Dynasty, Mandingo leatherwork, a Gupta Buddha—artifacts which could not be valued because of their immense social and historical significance, as well as their artistic merit. And at the far end, the Nacre landscape Aquilon had painted, at last in the appropriate company.

The fourth room was a library of first editions, the finest volumes produced by man. Every author, every researcher he valued was there, every book in perfect condition though some like the Caxton *Le Morte d' Arthur* were centuries old.

"And finally the chamber of Life and Death," Cal said as they returned through gallery and treasure-rooms to the hall. He opened the last door.

Armies were arrayed on either side: on the left a Roman phalanx, on the right the mounted horde of Ghenghis Khan. Subble had wondered idly, just as he was sure all agents wondered, what would be the outcome of such an encounter. The Romans had been supreme in their day, owing this largely to their discipline and training, but the Mongols of later centuries were a horde in name only: they were actually among the most methodical fighters and slaughterers of all time. Numbers being equivalent, the nomad riders were probably superior to any military

force prior to the advent of firearms, and had they
had rifles. . . .

Still, nothing was certain until the armies actually
met. Generalship was a vital matter, and morale, and
circumstance.

As the two visitors emerged from the hall, the
horsemen charged, screaming and firing arrows from
horseback while the Romans advanced stolidly,
shields overlapping, long spears thrust forward.

Cal was looking at him questioningly, and then he
remembered: the phalanx was not Roman, but Greek
and Macedonian! He was guilty of another careless-
ness, and now this anomaly was engaging the enemy. Exactly how *was* the Roman legion armed and
organized? The short sword, flexibility—

"This is visual, auditory and olfactory only," Cal
said, mistaking his concern. "The images will pass
through us without effect, or vice versa."

It was good to know. The armies met, and Subble
found himself in the midst of a savage engagement.
The horses reared up against the massed shields,
striking them with their hooves and beating them
back with the weight of their bodies. One hoof struck
at Subble, passed through him, and churned up turf
and sand. The brown-skinned rider swung his
curved blade at a break in the phalanx and the
Roman fell, his ear cut off. A spear lashed out,
lodging in the belly of the horse, and the rider came
down as gore spurted.

Then it was an indecipherable melee, suffused
with the stench of blood and iron and sweat and
urine and crushed vegetation, the screams of animal
and man, the sight of carnage and agony. Subble was
acclimatized to violence, but the brutality of this

encounter disgusted him. And he *still* wasn't certain whether the Romans had ever employed the true phalanx, or whether the Mongols ever stayed put for a pitched battle. The violation of history, after allowing for the basic anachronism of the situation, was probably worse than that of the slaughtered men.

Cal drew him back into the hall and closed the door. The bloodletting was cut off abruptly. "Come and relax for a while," he murmured. "I have some questions."

The end of the hall opened into a twentieth-century living room, air-conditioned and with the FM playing soft music. Subble realized with a start that it was the same piece he had heard at the intensive farming unit he had toured with Aquilon. The animals were pacified by music—and drugs—while they girded their corpulence for the butcher-machine.

"Please describe to me what you experienced," Cal requested.

"You weren't watching?"

"I wish to make a point."

Subble described in detail what he had seen in each chamber, a little embarrassed about the last. He was sure Cal would have some pointed corrections to make.

"Your verses differ from mine," Cal said. "You are still clinging to your own expectations. This is what I warned you against, and one reason I brought you here. It would be disastrous if you strayed this far during a meeting with the manta. Clear your mind of everything and follow me, and this time I will show you the true nature of the third kingdom." The little man was becoming more and more didactic, but Subble accepted the rebuke and accompanied him back to the fourth chamber.

It was empty. "Look at the ground," Cal said.

Ground appeared then: rich, dark earth. "See that mushroom?" Cal suggested, pointing.

A single mushroom sprouted, bursting from the soil in accelerated motion and opening its soft umbrella, white and delicate. "This is a saprophyte," Cal said.

"A saprophyte—an organism that feeds on dead organic matter," Subble agreed. "This is a characteristic of the mushroom and related fungi, while others are parasitic."

"Think about it."

Then Subble made the connection. Fungus—a thing that took its life from death, locked behind the door of Life and Death. This was a much neater definition than his vision of battle had been. And he had worried about military detail! Fungus—and Nacre was a world of fungus forms, to the exclusion of chlorophyll plants. Death—and Cal was obsessed with it, personally and philosophically. The genie Myco, whose name meant fungus; the hallucinogen, derived from another variety of fungus.

And the mysterious third kingdom itself—

Animal—Plant—and Fungus! Animals were animate, possessing, among other things, the powers of motion and conscious reaction. Plants performed photosynthesis, drawing nourishment from inorganic substances. But fungi neither moved nor drew energy from light—yet they lived and thrived. They had found an alternate route, and some experts— mycologists—considered them to represent a kingdom of their own, distinct from plants.

A kingdom that had ousted plants, to become dominant on Nacre.

"Forget about Nacre, for now," Cal said. "I want to show you what the third kingdom means to Earth. Mushrooms, fungi, mold, mildew, yeasts, bacteria—a little more heat and humidity and this kingdom would dominate right here. Fungi can live off almost anything organic: meat, vegetables, milk, leather, wood, coal, plastics, bones. The strains adapt rapidly. Develop a new jet fuel, and before long you will find a fungus feeding on it. The spores are tougher than we are; cold will not kill them, heat must be extreme to damage them all, dehydration—they can be dried and saved for years and grow again when conditions change. Fungi can grow at phenomenal speeds. Some are, as you know, parasites—their food doesn't *have* to be dead. Some change back and forth. One fungus can release hundreds of millions of spores in a few days—and those spores are everywhere, floating invisibly in the air we breathe and settling upon every mouthful of food we eat, no matter how 'clean' we think it is."

"In other words, they are pervasive," Subble said. "But at least they are under control, here." But he remembered the infestation of the cellar-farm, and wondered.

"That is a matter of opinion. Man cannot exist without them, while the fungi can certainly exist without us—in fact, without the entire animal kingdom."

"Evidently my programming isn't up to date on this subject," Subble said. "How is a parasite or saprophyte to exist without animals, live or still, to feed upon? And in what way am I personally dependent upon that little mushroom or its brethren? I can eat it, if it isn't poisonous, but I certainly don't have to, and I wouldn't miss it much if it vanished forever."

"To answer your first question: parasites and saprophytes cannot exist in isolation, naturally, but the plant kingdom is sufficient for their dietary needs, so animals are unnecessary. The answer to the second is more devious—but also more important, because *both* plants and animals are now dependent upon the fungus kingdom. Are you familiar with the oxygen–carbon-dioxide breathing cycle?"

"Of course. Animals take in oxygen and release carbon dioxide. Plants require carbon dioxide for photosynthesis, and give off oxygen. It's a rather neat balance."

"No. It is not neat at all. Animal respiration provides only a quarter of what is needed by the plants."

"A quarter? That doesn't add up."

"The rest is a by-product of decomposition."

"And decomposition—"

"Is the service performed by bacteria and fungi. Without these, dead organisms would remain as they died, sterile. Their elements would never be returned to the earth or atmosphere. Three quarters of the carbon dioxide, among other things, would be permanently trapped, the percentage growing, and the plants would be on a one-way track leading to extinction. And with the end of the plant kingdom—"

"The end of the animal kingdom. I follow you now."

"And without decomposition, no higher creature could have evolved on Earth. There would be no regenerative cycle; the first micro-organisms that ever formed would be with us today, two or three billion years dead but as durable as stone. Natural selection would never have had a chance. No room, no food, no air. As a matter of fact, to the best of our present knowledge, the presence of fungi of some type is essential to the development of *any* higher forms of life anywhere."

Subble looked at the mushroom with new respect. "I congratulate you, little saprophyte."

Cal led the way to the third door, that had previously opened on money, gems, works of art and a library. Again the room was blank until he spoke.

"You saw wealth in conventional terms. Most people do. But in reality, wealth is not money, art or literature; it is the improved standard of living these things represent. A man can starve, locked in a roomful of gold, or in a library. The gold must be traded for functional products, the books interpreted to apply to tangible things. What you saw were the convenient *symbols* for wealth, material and intellectual—handy for tabulations and comparisons and storage, but not directly contributory to personal well-being."

"No argument there," Subble said. This certainly *was* a lesson in how far afield a mind could go when not corrected.

"Instead, let's look at the things we can *use*. Observe the healthy expanse of growing barley, wheat, rye and oats—the breadbasket of a nation, a world."

Subble saw the patchwork of fields as from an airplane, stirred like standing water by vagrant breezes. "And peas, tomatoes, onions, potatoes." The plane swooped low to bring these into view. "Cattle, sheep, horses." Livestock ranges appeared—the old kind, before the animals were herded into darkened buildings for confinement and forced feeding.

"But these are ordinary plants and animals," Subble pointed out.

"But they are dying. See, the leaves are wilting, the animals are feeble." And they were; a massive blight swept over the fertile scene, destroying flora and fauna alike.

"They have been attacked by tiny eelworms, nematodes," Cal explained. "We are shrinking now, rapidly, down to rat size, mouse size, insect size—but the destroyer is neither rodent nor insect."

The airplane vanished and the fields zoomed closer, as though they were falling, and expanded voluminously. Then the two men stood on the ground and watched the world explode around them. "We are an inch tall, a tenth of an inch, a hundredth."

The world was an animated microscope slide. "We are in a chamber in the soil, the humus just below the surface. This is the most active biologic zone of the world, the vital key to the entire ecological cycle. This is the fiercest battleground of the three kingdoms—they fight ruthlessly, you know—and there are monsters here more astonishing than any we know in the macrocosm." He gestured. "Before us is one such: the nematode, the most successful wormlike organism on Earth."

Subble looked at it: an eyeless python twenty-five feet long, according to present perspective. The semitransparent body behind the bare oral openings was a foot in diameter. "It eats anything, but especially root hairs," Cal continued, "and it can lay its own

137

weight in eggs in a week. It is one of the most savage destroyers we know of, and the plants we cultivate have little effective defense against it, since we corral them in so tightly. A cultivated field is like an open supermarket, for the worm."

The nematode slid toward them, its body slimy and rank. Subble stepped back. "Do other animals handle it satisfactorily?"

"It would dominate the world, if not stopped— and neither plant nor animal seems capable of controlling it. It parasitizes larger creatures, too. It can expand its length a thousandfold, in time, in the intestine of a mammal. No sizable crops would survive its ravages, and—"

"I understand the gravity of the situation," Subble said, retreating another step as the blind orifice quested after him. "Just what *does* stop it?"

Cal pointed to the side. "Now here is a handsome clump of saprophytic fungus. Perfectly harmless— we can pass among the threads—the mycelium— without danger."

"Third kingdom to the rescue!" Subble said, climbing through the spongy brush he pictured. At least it offered some tacit resistance to progress of the hungry worm. But the nematode remained intent on their trail, and forced its way through the mycelium close behind.

"But you see, the nemin coating the creature's body has a peculiar effect on the fungus. As soon as a nematode approaches, short branches sprout with loops at the ends." The loops appeared, each about a foot in diameter. The worm ignored them, thrashing after the retreating men with almost mindless determination. Subble still did not feel at all comfortable so close to its eagerly sucking mouth.

But the loops became so profuse that they were unavoidable. The men pushed them aside, but the nematode didn't care; it poked its front end into one and came on, sliding through it easily. But the thicker central part of its body jammed; the loop was just too small to permit free passage. The creature struggled, attempting to withdraw or squirm on through the construction—but the loop inflated like a rubber tire and pinned the worm securely about the middle.

Now there was furious thrashing. The monster whipped its head and tail back and forth with frightening violence, but the booby-trapped ring only bound it more tightly. The nematode was far larger and heavier than the fungus, but it was not anchored and its leverage was poor in this position. It was unable to break the narrow band.

Gradually its struggles diminished, and it expired.

"Some species of fungi touch sticky knobs to the worm, holding it down, then grow strands into its body to consume its innards. Others deposit spores that germinate and parasitize it," Cal said, watching the dying worm dispassionately. "In any event, it is indeed the third kingdom that saves our crops, in this important instance, and so is the protector of our wealth, much more significantly than your hoard of gold. It kills animal parasites, and in many cases sets up symbiotic relationships without which even mighty trees could not flourish. We have just seen an omnivore fall prey to something it didn't even notice was dangerous, but that is only one aspect of the story."

That was significant. An omnivore brought down

by a seemingly innocent fungus. Even through the layers of hallucination, he perceived the stress Cal placed upon the concept. Man's appetite was very like the worm's. "Evidently you have been researching the matter."

"I reviewed it, at any rate. After Nacre, I had to. The representatives of the third kingdom are primitive, here, perhaps because there is always food for them and further evolution is not essential to survival—but they remain the best key to the advanced species there. I haven't begun to cover the economic importance this kingdom has for Earth. We use molds in industry to synthesize the acids employed in the manufacture of plastics, new paints, photographic developer, bleach, ceramics, monosodium glutamate . . . fungus to break down petroleum and detergent . . . electric batteries powered by yeast action. And the wealth of knowledge provided in the laboratory: molds and bacteria are the most primitive organisms containing DNA, the basic molecule of life."

"Wealth indeed," Subble said, impressed. The DNA/RNA researches were leading to tremendous breakthroughs in the life sciences already. "But I'm not certain how this will help me to complete my mission."

"It is not my place to tell you that," Cal said soberly. "But my hope is that somewhere in this demonstration you will discover the clue I couldn't. We should be better able to understand the advanced fungi once we study the primitive ones. I'm afraid we made a bad mistake on Nacre, but I can't bring myself to define it and have no idea how to undo it. That is what you have to learn—and I think only the manta can complete the picture for you. You must learn to communicate on its terms, as you are now learning to do so on mine."

"So I understand." And that would be the reason for the drug. Cal could have presented the material directly, but not the experience of the hallucinogen, the training in personal submersion in order to respond to another person's slightest concept. With an alien, there might be no standard communication, and the nuance response would become all important. He was mastering the technique now—but he certainly would not have wanted to practice while facing the manta.

"Let's check the other rooms," he said.

They expanded to normal size. "Was it not a mushroom Alice ate in Wonderland, to change her size?" Subble inquired, requiring no answer. The third kingdom was pervasive, now that he had become aware of it as such.

"Health," Cal said at the next door. "Most people are aware of mycotic infection—ringworm, athlete's foot, histoplasmosis—but don't realize how much more they owe to fungal antibiotics and drugs. You saw an array of healthy people—but how many would have stayed that way without penicillin and the other fungoid derivatives?" He opened the door.

A foul odor wafted out. The chamber was filled with a monstrous bubbling vat, churned constantly by a mighty paddle wielded by the grinning genie. "Surprise!" Myco cried. "This is where I live."

It was penicillin mold, stimulated to grow in aerated nutrient fluid.

Cal closed the door, cutting off the smell. "Not to mention the work still being done with yeasts in connection with radiation sickness and cancer and memory restoration."

"Or with mental health, via the mind-opening drug therapy," Subble added. "That's a little fungoid trick I will not forget in a hurry."

There was a clap of laughter from the health chamber; Myco, it seemed, appreciated the feedback.

"Or mental control," Cal murmured. "Knowledge does have its dangers."

They stood before the door of the chamber of food. "Let me guess," Subble said. "Edible mushrooms of splendiferous variety: morel, puffball, shaggymane, polypore, truffle ... and breads leavened, liquor fermented, cheese ripened, all by virtue of yeasts and fungi cultures."

"Only partly," Cal said, smiling. "I could add the biblical manna from heaven to your list, since that was another fungus product that people have eaten directly in time of need, but I was thinking along another line. Actually, it is not necessary to give up your original banquet. I can double or triple it via the third kingdom."

"By feeding mushrooms to livestock?"

"By feeding garbage to yeast."

"Don't open that door!" Subble exclaimed. "The penicillin was bad enough. Let me remember my banquet as it was. Just tell me about it."

This time Cal laughed. "The processing is rather interesting, but I admit there are uncomfortable elements. Even our sewers have become marvelous fonts of nourishment." But he dropped his hand from the knob.

"Today there are six billion human beings on

Earth, and not more than ten percent are actually hungry. We're feeding our population better than ever in spite of its appalling growth rate. You can't do that on steak, no matter how brutally you intensify your farming. A steer yields less than a pound and a half of dried beef for every hundred pounds of feed provided it, and it takes many months to do it, and copious rangeland if you insist on a really healthy product. Much of what those impacted livestock batteries turn out is technically unfit for human consumption: tasteless, nonnutritive meat contaminated with residual insecticides and deleterious hormones." This seemed to disturb him more than the idea of food from sewage.

"A pig yields six pounds of pork for the same bag of feed, and does it in less time and much less space," Cal went on. "But still there isn't room or food for the porcine billions that would be required to feed us if that were the major dietary staple. Other animals are no better. Plants are more efficient as food converters—barring nematode infestations!—but there is only so much arable land. We use artificially illuminated interior farms, multi-leveled, certainly, and we also farm the sea and to a limited extent the atmosphere—but our biggest single source of protein today is torula yeast."

"*Yeast?* Straight?"

"Not exactly the variety that makes bread rise," Cal said. "But the principle is the same. Torula feeds on almost anything organic—refuse from sawmills, molasses, rotten fruit—even petroleum and cool tar."

"Another omnivore!"

"You could call it that, yes. It produces sixty-five pounds of edible solids for every hundred of feed,

143

which is ten times as good as any animal, and what it consumes is foodstuff that would otherwise be largely wasted. And it does it on no more land area than that required to support the vats, multiplying its original weight many times in a single day. It can be mixed with other foods, indistinguishable by taste and rich in nourishment. Half of what we eat today is in fact processed from varieties of torula—and the average man doesn't realize it. Your turkey, your stuffed pig—if those were standard brands, much of their weight was textured and sculptured torula protein. A lot of artistry goes into blending it."

"It must," Subble agreed, "if the banquet in my own imagination is made from fungus I didn't know about!"

"You're in good company. Our spacemen are fed their own waste products, broken down by the yeast. Anyway, *this* is the true breadbasket of the world—and man can no longer survive at his present level without the generous assistance of the third kingdom."

They mounted the steps and emerged upon the terrace. "That's it," Cal said. "That's what the third kingdom means to Earth. Remember that Nacre is an advanced fungus world; it is billions of years ahead of us in that respect. Somewhere in all this information is the key to disaster, perhaps, for all of us." He stooped beside the lamp, still quietly burning, and snuffed out the little flame.

Almost immediately the nether staircase faded. "No residual effect?" Subble inquired, indicating the lamp.

"Not with this dosage. You would not want to overdo it, however. None of the hallucinogens are

mere amusements." He considered for a moment.
"I'm not sure what would happen if a person ever
became entirely subservient to this drug. It isn't ad-
dictive, theoretically, but it's potent stuff. We sat
about a yard from it, which diluted it sufficiently,
but if you inhaled directly over the flame—"

"My antibrainwash syndrome could trigger self-
destruction," Subble finished.

"Yes. It would in effect give you a psychoneurotic
disorder, and you haven't been conditioned to it as
we have."

"You showed me all this for a reason—not just
background or practice. What reason?"

Cal would not meet his gaze. "I lack the courage
to tell you. I hope most urgently that I am wrong—
but you must discover that for yourself, then do
what you must. Perhaps you will find, incidentally,
some solution for our more personal problems."

Subble nodded. "I promised to help Aquilon, too.
That's really the price for your cooperation. I'll do
what I can. But first I'll have to take your lamp and
your communication device and go to meet the manta directly. That is where it will end."

"I don't know whether to wish you success or
failure."

"One other thing," Subble said. "I want your segment of the Nacre adventure. I only have part of the
story so far."

"Yes—there is that," Cal agreed wearily. "I had
forgotten. We'll have some torula pancakes and . . ."

*　　*　　*

Hours later, away from the stench and gore, they
camped on another thin ledge and spread out on the

ground. Veg and Aquilon were tired, and quiet for their own reasons; the manta was as inscrutable as ever. It had fed upon the omnivore's carcass, absorbing the juices through its digestive underside, and now seemed content to relax. Aquilon had looked at the remains and decided to continue eating fungus after all. Only Cal was possessed of new strength.

"Do you know," he said, "that manta must be the most formidable fighting machine on the planet! Did you see the way it cut apart the omnivore? Our rifle didn't faze the monster, but the knife-edged tail of the manta slashed it to pieces. And the omnivore knew it; it was afraid."

"We—didn't see all of it," Aquilon said. "But why doesn't the manta attack *us?*" Her motive seemed to be more to encourage him than genuine curiosity. "Why does it keep Veg away from me, and not from you?"

"I've been thinking about that," Cal said. He was buoyed by some nameless excitement, as though the horrible encounter had released him from a geis. He would have to explore the reason. Could it be some invigorating chemical in the omnivore blood he had eaten—or had the revelation of his vice brought relief instead of shame? No, there was something else, something highly significant, that he could not pinpoint yet. "I've also been wondering why the herbivores weren't afraid of the manta. And I think I have the answer."

Veg stared morosely into the ground, facing away from Aquilon. Something had passed between them, something Cal didn't know about, that left both pensive. But what? There had been no time for any private dialogue, and the battle with the omnivore should not have prejudiced their interpersonal relationship.

The entire complexion of their little group had somehow been changed. Veg had been dominant at the beginning of the adventure, running the tractor and determining their route back toward the camp. Then, with the slaughter of the first manta, Veg had given way subtly to Aquilon, the artist and anatomist. Now the immediate problems of survival for the three of them had been surmounted, and their eventual return to the base seemed probable—if they could grasp the special nature of their contact with the manta. Obviously it could kill them all, and might do that, if they gave it incentive. Now was the time for intellectual exercise, for problem solving on other than a physical basis. Now it was Cal's turn to be dominant. But that was not the source of his exhilaration.

Aquilon was curious. "You can explain the manta's actions?"

"I think so. But it's not simple, and the implications may not be pleasant."

"I think we'd better know," Aquilon said. "If it affects our safety ... and it isn't as though there hasn't been unpleasantness already."

Cal looked at her, concerned for the effect his words might have upon her. She was a very sensitive girl. He glanced at Veg, but knew the big man would shrug off the implications. "It does affect our safety—and our pride," he said. "On Nacre, the ecological chain seems sparse: one species of herbivore, one of omnivore, and also, apparently, one of true carnivore. But that's only a very small part of the story. It is impossible for animal and fungoid life

147

to exist to the exclusion of the photosynthesizing plants. Those are the ones that manufacture food from light and inorganic substances, using chlorophyll, the green pigment. Everything else feeds on these, directly or indirectly."

Veg began to take an interest. "None of those here."

"They *are* here, though. They have to be. They're in the atmosphere, microscopically small, circulating in the higher reaches where sufficient sunlight penetrates. As a matter of fact, the evidence is that the major ecological chains are completed in the atmosphere, and that the ground is merely a wasteland for the debris. Thus the plant life remains primitive, since it can't establish a ground base, send out roots, form a woody structure, flower and so on. It is like plankton in Earth's sea, floating and growing where conditions are favorable, and falling to the bottom when it grows too large to remain suspended. That's our dust—the perpetually sinking plankton. The plants really seem to occupy a subordinate niche here, perpetually retarded, just as many fungi are on Earth. That's an oversimplification, of course—"

He saw their restlessness and realized he was lecturing. "At any rate, the ground habitat is restricted enough so that three major species of animal have been able to dominate, at least in the section we have seen. The so-called herbivores feed on the dust, and are easy prey, but without them the other species would perish. It would be easy for the omnivore to wipe them out, seemingly—"

"But what about the manta?" Aquilon asked. "It should be even more—"

148

"Let him talk," Veg growled. Nettled, Aquilon shut up.

"The manta, the true carnivore, would maintain the balance by preying on the omnivore, which in turn eats anything available, from dust to men. But the manta shouldn't require the herbivore for food at all—"

"That's it!" Veg exclaimed. Aquilon gave him a look. "The manta doesn't eat herbies. It protects them!"

"Let him talk," Aquilon said.

"If I'm right," Cal continued quickly, "these creatures would instinctively define everything in terms of their own system. There would be just three animal classifications: herbivore, omnivore and carnivore, preying, respectively, upon no creature, upon all creatures, and upon just one: the middle. So the herbivore would have to fear only the omnivore, and might even be protected by the manta. They would distinguish each other by type, not physical appearance, since their shapes are somewhat flexible—and may even be able to distinguish similar divisions in unrelated species. As fate would have it, the three of us represent—"

The other two came to life. "Herby!"

"Omnivore!"

"And carnivore," Cal finished. "In that light, the manta's motives are clear. To it, Veg is a helpless creature in need of protection. Every time a manta has seen him, it has followed, probably in response to that impulse. Naturally it has to safeguard him from the menace so close at hand."

"It was protecting *him* from *me*," Aquilon said, not entirely pleased.

"That time in the herby herd," Veg said, running it down. "The manta sailed right over me. It could have sliced me in half with that tail, but it was headed for her. And when that omnivore attacked, our manta didn't budge until I got in the way. It must've figured Cal could take care of himself, and it didn't care about 'Quilon. . . ." He paused. "And I killed the first one. It was trying to help me, and I shot it down—"

"It might have killed 'Quilon, otherwise," Cal reminded him.

"But why," Aquilon said, beginning to comprehend her personal danger, "why didn't this one attack me right away, instead of watching?"

"It must have realized that all three of us were alien," Cal said, finding the need to offer something though this question bothered him considerably. "It may not know quite how to deal with us, and is holding off until it can make up its mind."

"Still no call to cut the alligator pack-straps," Veg muttered.

"Don't you know the difference between alligator and granulated pig leather?" Aquilon demanded. "Those straps are omnivore hide."

Veg looked embarrassed.

"After a rude surprise like that, no wonder it wanted to keep an eye on us," she continued.

"A large eye," Veg said, staring at it.

"But when it finally comes to a decision—"

"I suggest that we get back to the base before it comes to that," Cal said.

Aquilon looked at the manta's well of an eye and shuddered. Death stared back at her.

They climbed with new incentive. The manta followed, declining to take action—yet.

The trail ended in midafternoon. One moment they were toiling past coral cones and hanging yellow strings crowding the path in increasing proliferation; the next, they faced a vast level plain extending into the haze. To either side the fungus colored the brink, setting it off, but most species did not venture far onto the plateau.

Veg studied the compass. "Six miles. But we can't make it today."

"So close?" Aquilon asked him. "But why not?"

"We could make the level distance, all right. It's the up-down that bothers me. We must be a mile in the air. Got to be a drop-off somewhere. . . ."

"Oh."

"One more night on the road won't hurt us," Cal said. "Manta permitting. I'd certainly like to know just how smart this creature *is*."

"Smart as a man, you figure?" Veg asked.

"I didn't say that. We know that it has a complex brain, or something analogous, and its actions certainly show something more than blind impulse. But with its superb fighting equipment, it doesn't really need intelligence as we think of it. There isn't enough challenge. It *could* have genius, but—"

Aquilon's brush and canvas appeared. She seemed to have shaken off her apprehension about the manta. Once again the vitality of her personality showed in two dimensions as the brush created its extemporaneous color. Sitting before the manta, trying to conceal any nervousness she might have felt, she painted its portrait: the midnight hump of a body, the flickering depth of the mighty eye that transfixed her with unblinking candor, the cruel whip-length of the tail, now curled on the ground in a circle about its foot.

The manta sat through this, quite still.

"Try one of the omnivore," Cal said, understanding her purpose. Aquilon obliged, producing from memory an effective rendition of the charging monster. She presented it to the manta, but met with no response.

She tried a herbivore, a fungus, an enlarged manta eye, all to no avail. It would not be possible to establish communication unless she could find some point of reaction. At Cal's further suggestion she drew an omnivore charging at a group of herbivores. Still nothing. She went on to portray lifelike caricatures of the three human beings. Finally she drew a picture which she concealed from the men, showing it only to the manta. When that also brought no response, she hesitated, flushed gently, and signaled to Veg, who was getting ready to backtrack for the pack down the trail.

"Something I can do for you, Beautiful?" he inquired. Cal noted this with interest; apparently whatever had soured them earlier was fading, and the subdued flirtations were recommencing. Thus encouraged, Aquilon beckoned again.

Veg came—and the manta moved. Dust swirled as its flat body angled between them. Aquilon cried out and dropped the sketch, while Veg jumped back.

"Still forbidden," he commented sadly. "That thing sure watches out for what it thinks are my interests. Otherwise you know what I'd——"

His eye fell on the picture, lying face up on the ground. "Yeah, I guess you do."

Cal looked at it. It was a picture of Veg embracing Aquilon.

The following day opened with uneasy turbulence. On Nacre, the shrouded planet that sparkled in space like a pearl, the wind was seldom more than a wash of mist, and the day-to-night extremes of temperature fluctuated within ten degrees. There appeared to be no rain other than the constant fall of dust—yet on this morning something was developing, something very like a storm.

They moved on, traversing the last few miles toward the base. Veg's estimate was verified within two hours: there was a sheer drop at the other side of the plateau. The human base was so close that they could hear the distant clank of machinery, but it remained invisible in the mist.

The cliff was authoritative, here; there was no feasible way for them to scale it. A few puttylike fungi leaned over the edge, but did not brave farther. Veg shouted into the gulf, but without effect. There would have to be a detour.

As suddenly as it had come, the manta left. It sailed off the edge, spiraling down to disappear in the dust.

Veg peered after it, astonished. "It can fly," he said. Then his mind reverted to first principles. "Chaperone's gone!" He caught hold of Aquilon's slim waist and drew her close. He kissed her.

"Not bad," he said after a moment. "For an omnivore . . . maybe we *should* marry."

She kicked him and moved out of reach. Cal still

wondered what had caused the rift, now evidently healed and more than healed, but did not care to inquire. He felt no jealousy; it was enough that dissension had been removed.

With something less than enthusiasm they turned to the right and proceeded down a slight incline parallel to the cleft. Two miles to go—and they had had to turn aside.

An hour later they had to halt again. Across the sloping plain a thin line of disks appeared, emerging from the obscurity with astonishing rapidity.

"Mantas," Veg said. "Dozens of them."

"I'm afraid Ragnarok is at hand," Cal said. "Our guardian has returned with his company. If only we had been able to make some kind of contact." But he was not seriously worried; had immediate death been the verdict, the original manta would have handled it alone. This was something else, and therefore promising.

In moments the line of sailing creatures closed the distance and circled the human group. It was strange to see so many at once, after the three contacts with individuals. A single ring of them settled down, a manta every five or six feet, eyes facing into the center where the human trio stood. Most were sleek and black, though they were of differing sizes and variable posture. There was no way to distinguish one from another with certainty, since the shape of each body was not fixed, except by size. Cal could not even be sure that their erstwhile companion was among them.

"They found the one I shot!" Veg exclaimed. "They're here for revenge."

"I doubt it," Cal said. "How would they know

which one of us fired the weapon?" But that suggested a manta investigation, a trial. . . . "Probably they are merely curious how this weird collection of aliens manages to associate in harmony."

He hardly believed this now, and was sure neither other person was fooled. There was too much they did not know about these creatures. The mantas must have surrounded them for some purpose. Did they have a leader? A decision maker?

He spied a huge grizzled individual, two hundred pounds at least and almost five feet tall. Its eye bore upon him. Menacingly? Intelligently? Could size be an indication of status, since presumably the largest was the oldest?

Outside the immediate ring the smaller mantas moved about, leaping and cruising in widening spirals, their paths crossing and recrossing. It seemed to be an aimless pattern, antlike; and like ants, each member hesitated as it met another, exchanging glances and dodging by.

Cal observed all this with growing excitement. "That eye—why didn't I think of it before! It is constructed like an electronic tube, a cathode. It must generate a communication signal!"

"But why didn't my pictures—"

"I see it all now," Cal rushed on, hardly hearing her. "Why, more straight perception must be massed in that one optic than in all our multiple senses. It would be a highly effective natural radar device, emitting a controlled beam and coordinating the data returned. The dust would prevent confusion by limiting the range. I wouldn't be surprised if it detected depth by analyzing the time-delay of the returning signal."

"But if it could see that well—" Aquilon began.

"That's the reason! We see by our own 'visible' spectrum, but the manta wouldn't necessarily operate on that level at all. Even if it could make out the colors, it would hardly interpret them as a representation of a three-dimensional object. Its vision wouldn't utilize the same illusions of perspective as our own. You may have been showing it a flat, blank sheet."

Veg had been walking around the circle. "So it sees too well for us?" he asked.

"Partly that, but—" Cal drifted off, working it out. "We know from that dissection that virtually all of the manta's brain is tied directly to the eye. If it emits a modulated signal—why, its whole intellect is keyed in. Think of the communication possible, when two of them lock their gaze. The full power of each brain channeled through the transceiver . . . pictures, feelings, all of it in an instant. . . ."

"They must be pretty smart," Veg said.

"No, probably the opposite. They—"

Both stared at him curiously. He tried again. "Don't you see—so much of man's vaunted intelligence is required simply to transmit and receive information. Each of us has a wall of isolation, of ignorance, to transcend. We have no direct communication, and so we have to master complex verbal codes and symbolic interpretations, merely to get our thoughts and needs across. With such second-hand contact, no wonder a powerful cerebral backstop is necessary. But the manta must have virtual telepathy: one glance, and communication is complete. It needs no real intelligence."

"Yeah. Sure," Veg said dubiously.

The grizzled leader (presumed) swiveled to meet the glance of a traveling manta as a strangely hot gust of air washed over the assemblage. Then it was moving, and so were the others.

"There's something else going on," Aquilon said nervously. "I don't think they care about us. Not to talk with, anyway."

"If only we had the proper equipment here—a television transducer, perhaps—we might be able to establish direct contact," Cal said, disappointed. "We could photograph their signal and analyze it. But right now we have no way to know their motives." But he knew that she had a good point. It was a strange day in a strange area, and the strange actions of the mantas were more likely than not to be connected. Had the human party overrated its importance?

Across the plateau the gray mists parted. A brilliant light appeared, widening rapidly. The mantas scattered across the plain reacted with bursts of energy that tore up the ground.

"Look at them move!" Veg exclaimed admiringly.

The light expanded, sweeping toward them in a burning arc. "What is it?" Aquilon demanded, clutching Veg's arm. "That light—like a furnace. Where is it coming from?"

She realized what she was doing and jerked her hand away, but the sweeping shapes paid no attention. The mantas seemed possessed, darting about in a crazed firefly pattern.

More flares appeared, as far as he could see across the plain. It was a phenomenon that extended for miles, if what he observed were typical. Volcanic eruption? Then where was the noise, the earth-shuddering? This was silent light, flaring intermittently as though a curtain flapped before a projector.

Then he understood. "The sun—the storm has let in the sun!"

The advancing light struck one of the billowing fungi spotting the plain in this neighborhood. Almost immediately the structure began to twist and shrivel; then, as the radiation and heat penetrated its rind, the dormant gases inside expanded. The skin of the fungus distended in gross blisters; then the entire growth shattered.

"I never thought of that," Aquilon said, fascinated. "Nacre hardly ever sees the direct light of the sun. The native life isn't conditioned to it."

"Like a forest fire," Veg agreed. "Wipes out everything it touches, and nobody knows how to get away."

It occurred to Cal that this could explain the barrenness of the upper plain. The higher elevation might predispose it to such breakthroughs, letting the sun blast away all life periodically. Had the mantas come to warn them? Convection currents at the edges could keep enough new dust stirred up so that the fungus there was protected.

The sky opened near at hand and the terrible brilliance flamed down almost where they stood. Cal visualized the weight of the suspended plants becoming too great for atmospheric conditions, forcing an occasional massive inversion, just as sometimes happened in Earth storms. The overturning could become so violent, here where the lay of the land forced air currents up, as to create a rent from top to bottom and lay the ground open to the sun. But it could hardly last long; more ordered dust would soon fill in from the sides.

The mantas must have known it was coming. They had acted in foolhardy fashion, coming here for any reason at this time, unless the storm held some particular fascination for them. Now they leaped in masses over the edge of the fault, fleeing the blazing path of light.

"Look!" Aquilon cried, pointing. One manta had been trapped within the sunlit area. It cast about violently, unable to find shelter.

She started forward. "The sun is killing it. It can't see to get away!"

"There is nothing we can do," Cal cautioned her. "We can't interfere—"

"We can't let it die!" she cried. Veg caught her arm, but she knocked his hand away without even looking. He reached for her again, trying to restrain her, but she was away, running fleetly across the plain. She plunged into the sunshine without hesitation, straight toward the blinded manta.

In moments she reached it. The thing was writhing on the ground, and Cal could see the dangerous tail snapping without direction. It was trying to get its eye into shadow, but there was none.

Aquilon stopped briefly, looking at it. Cal knew the reason for her hesitation: she had never actually touched a live manta with her hands. Then she ripped off her light blouse and threw it over the creature's tortured eye. It would offer scant protection, but the idea was good. She circled both arms around its globular, contracted body and picked it up. Burdened with its weight, she ran heavily out of the light. The tail dragged on the ground behind.

Veg ran forward to help her, but she was already out of the danger area, putting down the manta. It was of medium size, or about fifty pounds.

The sun storm was over, as though it saw no point in continuing now that its victim was gone. Singly and in groups the mantas returned. Aquilon stopped to unwind the blouse from her manta's head. "I never knew they were cold-blooded," she said, as though that were the most significant thing of all.

The circle reformed. The largest manta came forward, and Aquilon stepped out of its way. It contemplated the quivering creature on the ground; then without warning it was airborne. The body of the blinded one shook as the tremendous disk passed over and cut it to pieces with invisible slashes. Soon there was nothing but a pile of tattered flesh.

"No, no!" Aquilon cried. She strained, but this time Veg's grasp was firm. She struck at him ineffectively, then fell sobbing into his arms. "I only tried to save it . . . did they think my touch contaminated—"

"Look out!" Veg shouted, throwing her to one side and lunging to the other. The great manta was coming, its fierce eye glittering. The disk seemed to expand enormously. Veg spread his arms as though to intercept and halt the creature by the mass of his own body, but it pleated in mid-air and funnelled by him.

Aquilon looked up—and screamed as the manta struck. Four times the tail knifed into her face before she could protect it with her hands. Then the vengeful shape was gone and she fell, knuckles to her cheeks, blood welling between the fingers.

160

Veg knelt at her side immediately, gripping both her wrists in his large hands and pulling her hands away by main force. Cal peered over Veg's shoulder, sick at heart. As Aquilon raised her face he saw her flowing tears mixed with the smeared blood. Cheek and jaw on both sides had been deeply slashed, but the blood was running, not gouting. Her eyes had not been touched, and no artery had been hit.

His gaze fell on her bare shoulders and back. The skin was red and beginning to blister from the brief exposure to the rays of Nacre's sun, the damage extending down to her bra strap.

Cal removed his own shirt, the need for cloth overcoming his extreme disinclination to expose his skeletal body. He handed it to Veg, who accepted it unceremoniously and wiped Aquilon's face as clean as he could. The cuts were sharp and well defined, not ragged, and the flow of blood diminished quickly.

"Need a clean one," Veg snapped; then, realizing what it was: "Hey!" He looked at Cal, embarrassed, then gripped the short sleeve of his own shirt and wrenched. Muscles bulged as the tearproof fabric tore. He moistened it with his tongue and carefully wiped away the remaining smears.

"I can do that," Cal offered.

"Maybe you'd better," Veg said grimly, remembering something. "I have business with Brother Manta." Rising, he strode to the rifle and picked it up, activating the flare-chamber immediately.

"No, stop!" Cal called, seeing his intent. "You can't judge the manta by our standards. We have no way to know its motives. It could have thought 'Quilon was responsible for torturing and blinding

161

that young one. They must have no real conception of the sun ... perhaps they even worship it as the embodiment of evil. They might even believe that we *brought* the light. . . ."

Veg paid no attention. He was stalking the large manta.

"They could even be right," Cal went on desperately. "Our ships go up and down, disrupting the atmosphere as we ferry supplies. Remember—man *is* an omnivore. . . ."

Veg stood still, holding the rifle ready, chamber hot. Cal knew the weapon could do a lot of damage as its steam fired a rapid stream of projectiles at the standing mantas. Its chief advantages were silent operation, except for the hiss of the escaping gouts of steam, and safe ammunition, since the motive power came from the rifle and not from explosive bullets. But it would be disastrous to fire it now; the mantas would very quickly realize its purpose and wipe out the attacker. A good weapon in the hands of an angry man . . .

"If *I* can live with the omnivore," Veg said, "so can the manta. She saved one from the sun—and that big bastard killed it and went after her. It tried to blind her. You saw."

"But she *didn't* save it from the sun!"

Aquilon looked up, startled.

"That manta had been blinded by the light," Cal said, hoping he could hold Veg's attention until he cooled off enough to remember he didn't believe in killing. "Remember, their eyes must be far more sensitive than ours, and the sun may be deadly to them. The first few seconds may have destroyed its vision utterly, as surely as though a glowing poker had been rammed into its eye. There would be no possibility of salvage, with such a delicate mechanism."

"But it lived," Veg said. "She saved its life."

Cal sat back and looked at him. "Life," he said. "You worship life. You think everything is all right so long as you do not kill—except maybe for revenge. You are a fool."

"I th-thought I was helping it," Aquilon said, putting her hand to her face to feel the wounds. She had not been seriously hurt; that was now obvious to all of them. The manta's attack had not been to kill—or, perhaps, to blind, either.

Cal shook his head, meeting her gaze. "You mean so well, 'Quilon—but you are thinking with your emotions, not your mind. Don't you understand— the manta *has* no other perception besides its sight. A man has eyes and ears and so many other senses that the loss of one doesn't really hurt him; he can function perfectly well with one or two impaired. You dissected the manta's brain two days ago; you know the eye is the only perceptory connection to speak of. Our own eyes are such feeble candles, ranged against that. But when it is destroyed—"

He took another breath. "When it is destroyed, the manta's *total contact* with its environment is severed. In such a case, it is only mercy to terminate its life quickly. Believe me, I know."

"Okay," Veg said, softening. "Now tell me why it went for 'Quilon. If it had so much mercy—"

"I'm afraid it *is* an animal," Cal said sadly. "Not capable of understanding that an omnivore is not necessarily an enemy. And yet—it could so easily have killed her. Those little cuts won't even mutilate

163

her face permanently. They're neat and precise, almost like surgery. A token punishment—"

"I don't think so," Aquilon said, speaking with difficulty. Her words were blurred as though she had trouble controlling her facial muscles. The cuts began to bleed again, and he hastily dabbed some more.

"Look!" Veg cried, still facing the main group. "Little mantas!"

The mass of moving bodies parted. It was true. There, herded by a grown one, were eight tiny mantas, the first babies they had seen. Their miniature leaps were uncertain, their landings awkward, and they had not yet learned to flatten their bodies properly for control in the air, but mantas they certainly were. They could not have been more than a few days old.

"They *did* understand," Cal said.

By expert snaps of her whiplike tail the adult drove them in a course that led directly to Aquilon. Cal got up and moved away. As they came to rest in front of her, the adult left. Mantas and humans waited, intent upon that scene.

Astonished, Aquilon looked down at the tiny group. From a six-inch elevation, eight sober little lenses looked back, flickering tentatively. Touched, she leaned over and spread out her arms, and the babies hopped into their circle trustingly.

"They are for me," she said in wonder.

"Too young to be afraid of the omnivore," Cal murmured. "Could a human mother ever show such trust? These eight will come to understand our ways. We'll be able to colonize, now. And—" here he

broke into a smile that set the years of agony aside—
"we shall come to understand *them*."

"For me," Aquilon repeated, holding the little
bodies.

"Don't smile, 'Quilon," Veg cautioned, then bit
his lip. Cal saw the motion and began to see what
had happened to make that joke unacceptable.

But Aquilon did smile. Gradually, in the reflex
suppressed for so many years, the corners of her
delicate lips upturned. Her face lighted, casting an
emotional radiance that touched man and manta
alike, reflecting from the watching eyes of all of
them. Now, unconsciously revealing the full extent
of the manta's gift—the physical pretext and the
psychological reality—she showed the beauty that
was in her heart unfolding like a brilliant flower;
warm and clean and fine, so full of rapture that the
onlookers were stunned.

IV. Wilderness

BUT THE LOVELINESS of a blooming flower may be a fleeting thing, Subble thought as he stroked through the water. Nacre had not solved any problems, it had only graven their names on heavier chains. So long as home was a ruinously impacted Earth, the horrors would remain in one form or another.

He towed a basket by a cord looped around his waist. A mile ahead rose the offshore key—a semi-tropic island preserved as a wilderness park, inhabited only by birds, rodents, arthropods and elements of the second and third kingdoms. It was dusk; the island was outlined against the sunset, black palm against red cloud. A few gulls wheeled, and there were sundry movements in the shadowed tide beneath him. That was all.

He swam, enjoying the feel of the cool gulf water, the slap of salty spume against his shoulders and face. There was discovery and danger ahead, perhaps death—but death was an impersonal thing to him. He had a mission, and its completion was at hand—whatever that might mean.

The story of Nacre ran through his mind. What an adventure it had been, for the diverse trio! A

vegetarian, a normal omnivore and a technical carnivore, solving the riddle of a world whose fauna
mirrored their own habits. Yet the solution had not
been complete, for now the deadly carnivores were
on Earth, and there was danger no one quite com-
prehended yet all suspected. Not the human problems of the male-female triangle; that would be
resolved quietly in its own fashion once the princi-
pals got together again. Not the risk of an alien
scourge on Earth, for the mantas were highly ethical
creatures; they *could* attack man, but would not.
They had come to comprehend, he was sure, not to
conquer.

What, then? There *was* danger, terrible peril. His
trained perception was suffused with it. Veg,
Aquilon, Cal—all carried the aura of fear, tied in
with the manta. There was a potent mystery to the
presence of the creature on Earth, and it was not a
matter of diet or savagery or even intent. The future
of Earth itself might hang upon the success of his
mission—and he still could not grasp *how*.

Early night, and the isle loomed close before him.
Subble turned on his back and looked up at the still
trees, and beyond them to the cold stars. He had
never been away from the planet himself, he was
sure; agents had to be specially conditioned for extraterrestrial duty, and there would be no point in
utilizing an Earth-trained unit for it. He understood
that the average man felt a nameless emotion when
viewing the stars, a kind of compulsive awe, a yearn-
ing to reach them and also a deep loneliness. Subble
felt nothing except a mild intellectual curiosity.
Probably he had been conditioned to cleave to
Earth, and could not leave it without suffering from

the same kind of emotional malady the normals suffered just existing upon it. Or perhaps it was because he needed no sense of continuity, of time-lessness, since he had no past and no future. There was only the mission, and the stars were elsewhere.

There had been other missions before, but no trace of them remained with him. He might have had severe adventures in prior assignments, and could be fated for worse ones to come—but such speculations were hardly worth the effort it took to dwell upon them now. Death did not frighten him, and neither did the termination of his mission. Failure was the only spectre, and he was not a man to fail easily.

No, there was one realistic fear for him. Sometimes, he knew, an agent became stranded. For some reason it might be impossible to complete the assignment and check in promptly, and an agent caught in that situation was obliged to continue indefinitely, gradually growing old and losing the edge of his powers, missing the automatic updating provided by the reconditioning. It could be due to a continuing relationship—marriage in the line of duty, for example—in which a substitution would be inexpedient. Of course, if a female agent happened to be involved. . . .

Occasionally there was an accident; the agent was reported lost in action and his file discontinued prematurely while actually he survived to strive futilely for termination. It could happen to him! The unit SUB could be incapacitated upon this island, unable to return or report, yet alive. It could be months or even years before a follow-up located him, during which period he would be without a mission.

The thought was horrible. His body was nothing, his life irrelevant; pain and pleasure were only commodities of existence. But the mission—that was paramount, and without it he was wasted. Waste was the only intolerable. Better a clean death in the line of duty; better by far.

His feet found the sand beneath the shallows, and he drew his basket to the beach. A score of tiny brownish fiddler crabs scuttled sideways away from him as he emerged. They disappeared into their peppered holes in the damp sand. He waited while one big-clawed giant, well over an inch long, tried vainly to get into two of the pencil-sized holes and finally squeezed into the third. He wondered whether the burrows were linked underneath, like Aquilon's residential section. Did they have air-conditioning and color television? Well, running salt water, perhaps.

The isle was quiet; no frogs or crickets chirrupped, and the birds held their peace. They were present, though; as he concentrated his faculties he perceived them all about, hearing their surreptitious motions and smelling their furtive animation behind the drifting odors of seaweed and rot. The animals would return to normal activities when assured he was not a menace. Already the fiddlers were peeking out.

It was a normal beach. The packed, even sand gave way to a line of tumbled larger shells just beyond the high-tide line: clam halves ranging from several inches across down to half-inch coquinas, broken red and white conches with the inner spirals exposed, bleached sand-dollars decorated with five-leaf clover designs. Farther back the weeds and creepers sprouted between occasional driftwood and dessicated palm fronds. Whitish morning-glory type flowers nestled upon beach-running vines, and toward the forest line the jointed, head-high sea-oats waved beside the great round sea-grape leaves.

He set up the electronic equipment and tested it. Cal's notion had been good: duplicate the frequency and quality of the manta's eye-beam and emulate the patterns of communication with the guidance of the oscilloscope. Cal had had limited success; he thought he had the proper channel, as it were, but had trouble gaining the cooperation of the mantas. Subble believed that the groundwork was good; now it was up to the faster responses of a trained man: himself. He would try it first without the hallucinogen; he was not convinced that this aspect of Cal's regimen was either appropriate or safe. There was no guarantee that the fungus drug would bring him closer to the representatives of the fungus world. It was as likely to give him the illusion of liaison, which was hardly his mission, and if, like an addict, he lost his perspective and inhaled an overdose—

It was dark when he finished, but this was no disadvantage. Subble, as a fully equipped agent, was at home in the night. He knew the mantas were largely nocturnal on Earth; they, unlike man, were severely handicapped by bright daylight, and only in the gloom of the forest or closed buildings could they function well. An overcast day might allow them to go abroad, however. It was not so much the sensitivity of the single eye as of the body: sunlight would burn away the delicate skin and interfere with the pressure responses essential to precision control of movement. This would be a fact of life for any creature with the properties of the manta; specialization inevitably brought special liabilities.

He was ready. Cal had said that the mantas would find him, once he made himself available—if they wanted to. They were half-grown now and knew their way about, preying on fish and rodents. They would come. After that—

Subble resigned himself to a long wait. If they did not seek him out tonight, he would look for them by day. It was pleasant enough here upon the spongy sand, contemplating the mosslike growths and ribbonlike weed—but the mission could not wait upon alien capriciousness.

There was no wait. They came over the beach, flying saucers kicking up gouts of wet sand, twenty feet apart. No evasion, no maneuvering; they came to rest in a wide circle around him, six one-eyed humps, now absolutely still, tails curled around their feet. The party was on.

He assessed each in turn, turning slowly in their cynosure. He had not seen any this close before, and had had only the descriptions of the three spacefarers to guide him, apart from the evanescent flash in Veg's woods and Aquilon's portrait. These were young individuals, smaller than the ones the trio had encountered; he judged their weight at forty-four pounds, plus or minus three percent. He was not yet certain of the specific gravity of manta flesh. The color was nongloss black. The six together would outmass him only moderately, and in this thin—for them—air their flight would suffer somewhat, requiring a greater spread for a given speed. Their eyes would suffer from increased signal-loss, too, since there was not so much atmospheric opacity to bounce it back. It seemed unlikely that they represented the physical threat to him that Cal had suggested, though he had come without his most formidable armament. Their concerted attack could be severe, however.

Subble had not come to fight. He was trained to assess the physical potential of any man or animal or machine he met, and this was an automatic process that signified no aggressive imperative. It was intellectual contact he required, on whatever level available. He turned on the communicator.

One manta hopped forward. A single bound, a single yard, and the tableau was as before, the circle broken only at that spot. Subble aimed the projector at the proffered eye and adjusted the settings.

Was all this paraphernalia necessary, he wondered? Surely the creature could read the nuances of human countenance by now with a facility impossible to any man or Earth machine. Selected frequencies probably penetrated the subject in the manner of an X-ray to read internal configurations, perhaps the convolutions of the brain itself. The manta might not have olfactory apparatus, but could actually *see* the minute particles arising from all objects, that men interpreted as smell. Sight could replace several of the conventional senses. This was sight quintessential, more potent than man's diversified hearing, smell, touch, balance, tension and fragmented other bodily perceptions. Sight, bringing almost total information, geared directly to the brain and thus the most efficient communicatory instrument ever devised or evolved.

But as Cal had theorized, this did not guarantee intelligence as man defined it. For man, communication was an effort; but the manta could convey its entire world-view in the blink of an eye. Not literally: the eye did not blink. The external lens seemed to be crystalline, requiring no lubrication; he wondered what mechanism kept it clean. At any rate, it could represent a barrier to increasing intelligence by its very effectiveness. Ants and termites had evolved complex societies without intelligence; instinct was more than sufficient. Mantas could easily have done the same, using neither intelligence nor instinct, but simply their version of complete communication.

Cal had hoped that he had discovered an alien civilization, but now, after further study, he was not certain at all. Cal wanted complete understanding, but had become resigned to the fact that he could not achieve it on his own, for reasons that eluded him. He had helped Subble as much as he could, though desperately afraid of the consequence.

Cal was not a man to be frightened by phantoms.

"Say something, Brother," Subble urged the manta.

The screen came to life. Meaningless patterns played across its surface, whorls and lines shifting in kaleidoscopic confusion. Meaningless to *him,* Subble reminded himself; the signals might be direct and plain if he could interpret them properly. Cal had succeeded in aligning the equipment to manta impulses, but the fine tuning still had to be done. This first step was equivalent to establishing radio contact while remaining ignorant of the language.

"Let's revert to sign language," he said. He brought out the light-pencil and played it over the separate photoelectric screen. Scribbled lines ap-

174

peared in its wake, as though he had run chalk over a blackboard randomly.

He hooked the screen into the main circuit and began to draw. He had, in effect, a two-way contact: his probe could initiate designs that were transmitted to the manta frequency, albeit crudely, and the screen would reflect impulses originated from the other end as well. Their minds could meet via this circumscribed channel—if the manta desired it.

"Observe." Subble drew a line of light and waited. The screen could only be activated by a steady, controlled impulse, and this had been demonstrated to be within the capability of the manta—when it chose to employ the technique. The transitory flickerings of the screen faded, indicating that the creature was following him, but there was nothing more.

He drew a second line beside the first. "Come on, whip-tail—make like an artist," he suggested. Still no response—yet the manta would not remain before the equipment unless it understood its purpose.

He added a third and a fourth line, and finally it happened: a fifth appeared.

"Now we're in business!" The manta was participating at last.

Subble erased the screen and drew a circle—and suddenly it was filled with duplicate circles and wiped clean again, with no action on his part. It was as tangible an expression of impatience as he could imagine. There was at least minimal comprehension, and phenomenal manipulative ability. "So you can make symbols," the manta had remarked, in effect. "So what? Stop wasting my time."

Could it simply have been tedium that had interfered with Cal's efforts? The little man was a deliberate thinker, checking and rechecking before taking any new step. Quite possibly the volatile manta had given up in disgust while Cal deliberated.

"I doubt it," he said aloud, finding it easy to maintain the one-sided verbal conversation while working out new lines of play on the board. That smacked of the same simplicity as the "revenge" motif when one of the mantas of Nacre had struck Aquilon in the face. The truth appeared to be immensely more complicated. The simple answer's main asset was its convenience for simple minds. There had to be more to the present problem than impatience—and already he had had far more specific success than Cal had described, despite his lack of experience with the manta.

"So you just didn't *want* to talk to Cal," he said, as his electronic pencil moved as swiftly as his heightened ability could control it. "Why not? Why do you speak to the stranger and not to your friend? Isn't that a little fickle?"

He drew a man, simplified and stylized but recognizable, he hoped. The manta produced an identical figure, seemingly instantaneously. Subble drew a flying manta and this too was reproduced.

Was he achieving anything? Mere imitation proved only that the line was open. He needed intelligent application, and he hadn't found it yet.

He drew a slightly larger man, and opposite it a Nacre herbivore. "You know Veg, right? And this is Aquilon, who brought you here, but didn't want to keep you all cooped up in her apartment. She's an omnivore—like this Nacre specimen, make of that

176

what you will. And this smaller male-symbol is Cal, who is—" He left the opposite space blank, and waited. If Aquilon's technique had been soundly conceived—

The manta figure appeared in the appropriate space. Success! It understood the parallel.

A dotted X appeared, superimposed over the entire screen, but the picture remained. Then, rapidly, a standard man-symbol appeared beside the female, and the herbivore and carnivore sets vanished. The manta was telling him that it knew that most men were omnivores; the screen quickly filled with human figures, the straight men and the bosomed women. But why the X?

Was the manta saying "I understand your point, but it isn't valid"?

Then the slate wiped clean again, to be renewed by a group of Nacre omnivores. Subble's estimate of manta intellect jumped abruptly as he watched what followed.

For the figures were animate, no longer stationary symbols. The omnivores quivered and pounced, horribly real, and now they took on color and a fungus background of the Nacre habitat. Their size expanded until the screen was a picture of a single living creature, leaping heavily and carelessly crushing the smaller mushrooms beneath its muscular foot.

A placid herbivore came into view, as though a television camera were centering on it—and the omnivore leaped upon it, tore away great juicy hunks of soft flesh with the toothed tail, and settled upon the spread remains to feed. Subble could even see the digestive acids flowing over the carcass, breaking the flesh down externally so that the predator's underside could absorb the jellied essence.

Then a single manta appeared, much smaller than the omnivore, but also much swifter. They fought, and the manta won and began feeding on omnivore meat.

The scene shifted to Earth: a recognizable tropical jungle. Subble now appreciated one of the reasons Cal had chosen to make his fungus commentary the way he had—in scenes. He must have suspected that the manta would employ this camera-mode.

A striped tiger prowled fretfully, the play of the great muscles beautifully pictured. A man appeared dressed as a hunter, with a heavy rifle in his hands. So accurate was the detail that Subble was able to identify the make of the weapon: one of the vintage gunpowder models. The tiger sprang; the man wheeled, brought up his rifle, and fired. The tiger fell and rolled on the ground, snapping and dying.

"Right," Subble said. "On Earth the omnivore prevails over the carnivore—and all other creatures. So long as he has his trusty technology at hand."

Now the picture split: the victorious manta on one side, the man on the other. The backgrounds metamorphosed into sand and palm trees: the island upon which they stood. The line between them faded. Man and manta stepped toward each other.

And the screen went blank.

The manta hopped out of the circle, past its companions, and found a place in the center of the beach. It waited. None of the others moved to utilize the electronic setup.

"Oho!" Subble exclaimed. "So that's the way the jet fires. You don't care to talk to me either."

He turned off the set. There was no use running down the battery until they settled this matter. The manta had proved beyond question that it *could* communicate—when it chose. It had gone as far as it intended to, and the next gesture was up to him.

Why? Because it did not respect the omnivore? Subble could understand this. He would be unlikely to treat a pig with respect unless the creature first demonstrated qualities deserving such attention. Unless, in fact, it were in a position to *command* respect—by superior intellect or physical prowess. Swine in a muddy pen were one thing; a great boar hog in the wilderness another. Wild tusks were more effective arguments than tame pork.

What did man have to distinguish himself? A technology that was superfluous to the framework of the manta, and rather crude where intelligible. Man's weapons were little more than an extension of the innate savagery of the species. Not an impressive total.

But Aquilon's act of faith and courage on Nacre had brought a limited response. That had been the first solid example of omnivore compassion the manta had observed and understood, and it had replied in kind. The seed had been planted.

Perhaps if the hunter saw the wild boar spare a human child, he would be constrained to hold his fire—but not necessarily to adopt that pig into his family. Respect had to be earned step by step; it could not be given as a gift.

The manta, it would seem, had returned Aquilon's favor and gone one step farther. It had sent its representatives to Earth. Now it was up to a designate of Earth to prove himself—step by step.

And the foundation had to be laid in the field of arms. The root of respect was almost always physical, no matter how tempting it might be to consider it otherwise. Man and manta had won their respective places by becoming the most deadly fighters of their worlds. The order of precedence had to be established before higher negotiations could begin. This was the essence of natural selection; not pretty, but necessary.

"So you wouldn't fight handicapped men," he said. "You insisted on a really capable specimen, so that there could be no excuses." That was why Cal had had no success.

The manta was waiting.

Subble looked at it. "Well, you've got one." Was he to pit his devastating physical attributes against a half-grown animal? Immediately he caught himself. He had just had formidable evidence that the creature was alert and sapient, yet he still thought of it as an animal. Acceptance was a two-way business!

Still it bothered him. Inherent in ritual combat was the concept of fair play, and this was evidently highly developed in the manta. They had not simply attacked him; they had explained first, and now awaited his acquiescence. Fine—but he was probably a match for several of the creatures facing him, while only one made the offer.

Subble's reflexes were keyed to speeds far beyond those of ordinary men, and his weapons were the finest Earth technology could provide. He was a superman; no creature on the planet could match his strength, speed, endurance and general command of combat technique—except another agent. These mantas, on the other hand, were adapted to another planet, used to a thicker atmosphere and a steadier clime. They should hesitate to commit their forces in unfavorable terrain, just as an agent like himself would consider it bad tactics to engage, bare-handed, a killer whale in the water.

Perhaps they had not completely understood the situation. He would clarify it.

"If you will direct your attentions to the inland vegetation . . ." he said, gesturing, but none changed position. One was already facing that way, however.

Subble's hands touched the band of his trunks. Two lances of fire appeared and disappeared. Two fronds on separate palm trees dropped to the ground, their blasted stems smoking.

Not a manta moved.

But distance weapons were not part of the manta's framework, though they evidently knew something about them. Subble stepped out of the armored trunks and dropped them beside the equipment. He removed his rather special watch, a potent ring, and certain portions of his bridgework. A naked man against a naked manta—that was closer to it.

"But it still isn't entirely sporting, Brother," he said. "You weigh in at forty-four pounds, no hands."

Subble moved: five steps, turnabout and somersault, in the time it would have taken an ordinary man to focus his eyes—and he had swept up a sturdy length of driftwood and shattered it with one blow of one hand.

The single manta waited.

"You offer me no apparent choice," he said regretfully. "I'll have to kill you before the others will believe." He knew there could be no mercy in

181

such a confrontation, for mercy in elementary battle was weakness.

He was prepared to do what had to be done, efficiently and supposedly without regrets—but he regretted this. His mission required the exchange of information with the mantas, to complete the picture, and a subsequent report. That was all—but they refused to cooperate until mastered. It was such a waste, to destroy an intelligent creature so casually—but necessary.

He strode to the center of the beach, fifty feet from the selected manta. As he did so the others bounded outward, taking up positions several hundred feet distant at either end of the long strip: two and two, with the fifth beneath the blasted palm on the inland side.

Subble paused, assessing the slope of the beach and testing the footing offered by the sand. He would do best to stay clear of the dry area, since that would be powdery and contain prickly sandspurs; he needed good leverage more than the manta did. Then he marched toward his opponent.

He was uncertain how to kill it cleanly. He could not expect to strangle it, since it did not breathe in any Earthly fashion, and the tail would be dangerous in close work. He could not expect to stun it with nerve blows because he did not know enough about its nervous system, which could be simplified and well protected. As a matter of fact, he realized belatedly, he knew much less about it than it knew about him. Perhaps the match was not so uneven after all.

The best choice, in the face of his ignorance, was a quick series of blows, crushing the head section.

The eye was the obvious vulnerability, and he did not wish to torture it by a slow death or dismemberment. The slaughter had a bad taste, but at least suffering could be minimized.

The manta did not move as he walked up. At twenty feet it looked pitifully small, an innocuous black hump with a single eye, something like a negative shmoo. Had he made an error? Had he misread its intent, and seen combat to the death where some gentler dialogue had been proposed? What a terrible mistake, if—

The manta was airborne, leaping away from him. He would have to catch it first—and one thing he could *not* do was outrun it. Even handicapped by Earth conditions, and under-age, it was probably capable of forty miles per hour over the sand. He would have to wear it down, or outmaneuver it, or mousetrap it as it assailed him. He was glad; it was too noble a creature to die ignominiously.

"The recipe for rabbit stew ..." he reminded himself. *Could* he catch it, if it stayed clear?

It angled into the air, a disk a dozen feet in diameter. The foot disappeared into the body in this attitude, streamlining it, and he could see the flux of the surface responding to air resistance. The thing was both kite and glider, as much at home in the air as on land, though technically it could not fly. Beautiful control.

The manta swooped at the ground—and suddenly it was coming directly at him at double its prior velocity. Subble threw himself prone, clapping one hand over the back of his neck and the other over his spine while his face dug into the sand. It passed over him, the tail striking down as he squirmed to the side.

He was on his feet again immediately, facing it, but the manta settled a hundred feet up the beach. He glanced at his hand, the one that had protected his neck, and saw a long shallow slash beginning just below the wrist and running eight inches down the forearm.

Then he knew what he was up against. The wound was not dangerous, and in moments his physical control had sealed it off almost bloodlessly. But it was at the wrong angle. The manta's tail, moving forward in line with its body, should have cut crosswise over his wrist. Instead it had sliced at right angles to the creature's flight.

The manta had not only had time to select its target carefully, but had had the control to make a rather awkwardly positioned cut.

There was a similar incision along his other arm.

It had returned Subble's warning demonstration: this pass had been to alert him to its capability, not to incapacitate him. Now they both knew where they stood.

It was probably the first time he had ever seriously underestimated his opposition, for he would not have been available for this mission otherwise. He had allowed for exaggeration in the Nacre episode, for the observers had had other concerns to distract them from really objective views, and he had allowed for his own surprise when the manta moved in Veg's forest. Now he knew that these reasonable allowances for human error were faulty. He was in a battle for his life, and it was not possible to anticipate the outcome.

The tail was too fast for him. After appreciating what it could do in a controlled run, he knew that it could crack the sonic barrier when snapped with force, just as a whip could. He had no defense but interference and avoidance. He had to keep the manta out of range while in striking position or it would blind him or slit his throat or lay open some other part of his body on the next pass.

The manta lifted, flattening as it gained speed, coming at him. Subble dived for the water's edge and scooped up a handful of pebbles. He whirled and began firing them as the disk approached, his throws rapid and accurate.

It dodged easily, rippling to let the stones pass harmlessly, but it slowed; Subble was aiming for the great eye and knew that should the manta grow careless and allow a hit it would be in serious trouble. He began feeding his shots in pairs, forcing double dodging, and abruptly the creature gave up and swerved aside.

The manta touched the sand and catapulted ferociously at him again. But this time Subble was not to be surprised; he leaped—high into the air, directly at the manta.

Its velocity was too great to allow it to swerve in time, and his body was far too big for it to dodge like a pebble. A collision would favor him, because he massed over four times as much as it did, and his body was comparatively bony. He reached to enclose it, knowing that its delicate extensions would be highly vulnerable to the grasp of his hands. The striking tail would be ineffective in the face of such direct bodily contact.

The manta flexed and passed under him, going

out to sea, and Subble landed on hands and feet, his nose not far from a pretty two-inch corkscrew shell lying just beyond the water. He jumped sideways and whirled, rearmed with stones, but the creature had not turned. It sailed over the rounded waves, the beat of its pumping foot casting up thin sprays of water.

Subble watched, startled, though he should not have been. Cal had remarked on this, and it was obvious that at the speed the foot struck, water was as good a medium for leverage as any. It was possible for a man to water-ski upon his two bare feet, if towed at sufficient speed, and the manta's foot-area at contact was far wider than man's. That was why they had chosen an island: the sea was a private highway.

But only at speed, surely. Were a manta actually to fall into the ocean, it would not be able to get up sufficient velocity to become airborne again, and its pusher would be virtually useless for swimming. That was worth remembering.

It was coming in again, flat and deadly as a flying knife. He could not hope to avoid it indefinitely; the manta was too fast, its tail too accurate. He could not run it down in his own time, either, since it could "walk" on water. If it became fatigued, it could cross to another island and recover at leisure; if he tried to swim after it, he would be subject to immediate attack in the water, where the disparity in their maneuverability would be greatest.

The manta gave him no time to think. It rose to an altitude of nine feet above sea level and sailed over the choppy waves of the incoming tide, too high for him to block effectively but just right for its own striking range.

Subble lurched to the side, and the manta shifted angles to head him off. But the mid-air maneuver cost it velocity that it could not regain without coming down. He ran along the beach, seeking the hard-packed wet sand at the very edge of the water and moving at thirty miles per hour: a feat impossible for any normal athlete.

The manta altered its course to follow him, touching the ground. It gained momentum. Subble heard it approaching, closing the distance between them rapidly. He could maintain this pace for only a few seconds, yet it was easily outrunning him. In a moment it would draw abreast, and the tail would flick across to touch the throat, the eye, perhaps the hamstring tendon above the heel, and he would be pinned for the kill.

It drew within ten feet. It was silent, except for the staccato beat of the great foot and a faint whistling of air. He positioned it by sound: two feet above the sand, six feet behind. It would have to get close, beside him or over him, to utilize the tail, unless it could whiplash over its own head. . . .

Four feet, three—and Subble stopped. He braked with all of his force, driving his feet into the sand and throwing back his body. His arms went up over his head, as stiff as ramrods, fists clenched.

But the manta too had profited from experience. At forty miles per hour it could not stop within a yard; its foot was structured for forward drive, not braking. As old Ettore Bugatti had protested when cautioned on safety: "I make my cars to go, not to stop!" Again Subble was using his less specialized physique to good effect; he could do more things than the manta could, even if he could not compete in its specialties.

It could not swerve aside in time, nor could it rise the six feet necessary to avoid him without totally disrupting its aerodynamics and looping out of control. It was made to go—but it had come prepared.

It accepted the collision.

The soft ball of it smacked into Subble's back— and bounced. He twisted around, grabbing for it again, but already it was bounding high into the air, ten feet, and opening into its traveling form, unhurt. One more trait had been revealed: the manta could protect its eye temporarily by englobing it in its own flesh, and its bonelessness prevented internal rupturing.

Why had it not done so in the Nacre sun storm? Probably because the light burned its skin and never let up; there it could not rebound and recover.

Subble scrambled beneath the spreading mantle, knowing that it lacked the proper leverage for a tail-strike when almost stationary. It was not the manta's own small mass that anchored it, but the resistance of the air to its spread body. That same resistance provided the real forward impetus, too— the foot pushed primarily *up,* but the sail tacked against the stable air and sent the body shooting forward much faster than otherwise. The manta was a creature of motion, and could not even achieve its full umbrella without sufficient velocity. Now it was almost still, and had to descend for at least one push before getting away. To this extent it had miscalculated.

And Subble was under it. "Come to Papa," he said as his hands reached up, enclosing the vainly fluttering shape. But he kept his face averted; it could blind him yet, as his grip on its body provided some of the vital leverage. He would have to fall upon it, crushing it into the sand, encumbering the tail—

A sledgehammer struck his head.

Subble fell, stunned by the blow. The shallow water came up to meet his face, and the bright shells under the surface, though the night was black. The manta had driven its foot at his head, perhaps instinctively, and almost broken his neck! His brain had been severely jarred; unless he brought his bodily reactions under control immediately, he would lose consciousness—and life.

And mission. The phosphorescent surface smacked against his face. It was sheer luck; the external shock stimulated adrenaline and gave him momentary control. He brought his knees up under him and pushed for deeper water.

Or was it Enrico Ferrari who made his cars to go?

The manta was coming again, ready this time for the kill. Its black shape passed a few feet to the side, visible only as a moving shadow. Subble placed it principally by ear, discovering that he had temporarily lost his infrared vision, more sensitive to damage than normal sight because it was artificially implanted. He was, in this situation, virtually blind.

A searing blade slashed across his shoulders, laying the flesh open. Painful, but not crucial—but the end was near if he could not get away in seconds.

Subble dived. The ocean was only four feet deep

here, but it was enough. The dread tail could not strike at him through very much water. He was safe—so long as he could hold his breath.

He could hear the foot pounding against the surface as the manta circled above, frustrated for the moment. It would slice away the top of his skull as soon as it appeared above water—but he would drown if he did not come up within another minute. He had good resources here too, and could ordinarily stay under a long time, but he had entered the water disadvantageously. Unless he could deceive the manta in some way, gaining time for a breath—

The shape passed directly over him as he continued to stroke out to sea. Subble lunged for the surface and gulped air before it could turn. The manta's liability here was that it could not remain stationary on the water; it had to keep moving, and that allowed a few seconds between passes. By the time it could return, he was below again.

But how long could he hold out? At best this represented a standoff, and at worst defeat for him, if the manta learned to time his rise for air and lash out then. He could not overcome his opponent by hiding from it. If he lasted this way until daylight—still many hours away—the creature would probably retreat to shade on another island. Then night would come again. . . .

The beat of the foot stopped. Subble listened, interpreting the cessation of the loud clear sounds conveyed by the water, and the strange substitution. The manta was coming at him—*under the surface!*

But almost immediately it was out of the water again, resuming flight. Now he realized what had happened: the manta had cut below the waterline much as a flying fish cut above it; a shallow, temporary incursion dependent upon initial velocity. This was a dangerous maneuver. One second too long, and it would be trapped, lacking the speed to angle successfully back into the air.

Why had it taken such a chance? Unless it could not locate him from the surface—

He worked it out. The manta was dependent upon one perception: sight. It was a phenomenal perception, but still subject to the limitations of the medium. It was necessarily narrow-beam; an eye which provided its own radiation had to limit its energy output stringently or essential resources would be drained from the system. Even a simple flashlight soon exhausted its batteries. Human beings, who utilized external sources of illumination, used as much as twenty-five percent of their bodily energies in connection with their eyes alone. The ratio would be worse for the auto-illuminants of Nacre, unless they were considerably more efficient.

But a narrow beam was virtually useless for locating a specific object in space. Even the wide-beam perception of Earthly eyes required special synapses to call motion to the attention, which solved most problems. A warty toad was lost amid the dry leaves of the forest floor, though in plain view—until it moved. Peripheral vision and sensitivity to motion: these were vital to a moving creature. The manta seemed to have neither; it played its fine beam over all objects and knew by its biologic radar what they were and how they moved.

What would the refraction of water do to this power? For man, the apparent displacement of objects beneath liquid, and the reflective properties of the surface were merely oddities and occasional nuisances. Man had other ways to plumb the depths. For manta—it could be a complex problem indeed. It had no verifying senses except the touch of foot and tail and skin, and these were almost useless here. Yet it was experienced enough to realize that the medium *did* effect the impulse, as a man might see a mirage and hear a ringing in his ears while knowing that these things did not reflect the true situation. Indeed, as a man might perceive a complete framework of stimuli, and know them all to be false ... as he had done himself under the influence of the hallucinogen.

As it was, that dialogue had disturbed him. Now he was uncertain about little things, such as exactly what a given racing-car pioneer had said. It *must* have been Bugatti!

So the manta could not trust what it saw beneath the shifting waves. Still, it could wait for the telltale appearance of his head above water—except that its narrow-beam vision made this largely a matter of chance. How likely was a man with a small beam to spot a figure in a dark ocean—a head that appeared only a second or two every three minutes or less?

The odds were with him after all! He could swim underwater and come up near the manta at any time—and duck when spotted. He could find a pole and jab it, spearlike, at the passing enemy, without emerging at all. No wonder the creature was desperate to locate him!

Subble broke surface and looked about. He was in deep water now, and had the whole gulf to hide within. It was still dark to his gaze; apparently his infrared was gone for the duration. He could compensate to a considerable extent, since that seemed to be the worst of his injury, apart from the slash across his back and a headache he was able to suppress. He could see the white beach and the tall stars; only the black on black of the manta evaded him visually. But he could hear it well enough, ranging at a distance, and smell its distinctive, funguslike aroma.

He had lost some blood and his neck was stiff; he had gained a major tactical advantage. He was, all in all, in good shape.

"Over here, Brother!" he called.

And the manta looped about and came toward him. It had heard!

Subble submerged hastily and sought a new location. How could a creature without auditory apparatus respond to sound waves? Cal had shown him a copy of Aquilon's dissection pictures: the manta had no ears and its skin was not attuned to sonic vibrations. It had only the eye.

Unless it could actually *see* sound waves. . . .

He could not chance it. Obviously it *could* locate him when he made a noise, and if it missed the tiny splashes of his lifting head in distant water, it would not overlook those noises near at hand, or the vapors of his breath. Impasse again.

He came up, spotting it near his last emergence. But as he did, it changed course and zeroed in on him. Once again it had profited from experience, recognizing the noises characteristic of him and watching for the expanding atmospheric waves that were his sounds. He had thrown away his major advantage.

Again, his choices were continuing retreat—or

death. This ocean episode had given him a limited reprieve and educated him somewhat, but it had not forwarded his mission particularly. Better to meet the foe on land, where, if defeat were more likely, so was victory. If only he understood the manta better!

And suddenly he did. The thing that Cal had hinted at and had not been able to say; the thing that made the manta incredibly dangerous to civilized Earth; the obvious rendered obscure by a mind trained to expertness at conventionalities—the pieces of the puzzle began to fall into place at last, and hinted at the devastating consequences of ignorance.

He took a breath and stroked powerfully for the cache of equipment. He stayed under as far as the diminishing depth permitted, then emerged silently, holding his breath. The tide was at its height, the surges almost touching the basket, but it was undisturbed.

Beside it sat a dark hump. The manta had anticipated him!

But it did not attack. He realized with relief that this was one of the watchers, a noncombatant. It would leave him alone—he hoped.

Carefully he knelt at the basket and drew out the lamp. He found a match—still the surest route to fire!—and thumbed it to life. As it flared the distant manta veered, aware of the sound or the radiation of heat or light or some other ambient characteristic of fire. He touched it to the spout of the lamp, willing it to catch quickly. It did, and he moved to the center of the beach, nostrils close to the flame.

The manta left the water and shot across the narrow beach, its eye bearing upon him with the typical flicker; he could see that much directly now. Subble readied a fistful of shells and pebbles, but it sheered away from the steady green flame. Did the hallucinogen affect it too? Or did it suspect some more subtle trap?

Subble inhaled, knowing he was taking too much but urgent for the drug to take effect, while the manta circled warily. Cal had been right; this was the only reasonable avenue for comprehension, in the circumstances. And he had to understand the creature before he dared to kill it.

* * *

The old one was dying. Laboriously it made its way to the place of decease, climbing the narrow trail though hardly able to spread its brittle aerofoil. Periodically it rested, its massive body sagging with fatigue, the eye staring lethargically. The younger, vigorous ones passed it in salute and went on, sparing it further exhibition of its incompetency. The last trip had to be alone.

The old one came at last to the highest plateau and collapsed ignominiously upon the level dust. It was the end—but life remained behind the glazed eye, flickering into the final configuration. Blind, the old one rose on its flaccid foot, the globe of its body swelling tremendously. The extinguished eye bulged and exploded; the body split asunder. A cloud of smokelike particles puffed into the air, spreading slowly through the staid atmosphere.

The body collapsed, an empty husk devoid at last of animation, awaiting only the periodic annihilation of the fire from the sky. No omnivore would defile the remains after that cremation. Life had not been destroyed; it had passed on, into myriad microscopic free-floating spores. The old one had contributed its genes to the world.

The spores ascended, diffusing as they drifted over the face of the cliff and caught the circulating breezes there. They traveled, half an octillion strong: five times ten raised to the twenty-sixth power, or a numeral followed by twenty-six zeroes. Their motions were random, within reasonable meaning of the term; they were governed by trace eddies and currents, and by the gentle static repulsion contributed by their common charge. They were male and female—that is, complementary half-chromosome arrangements—in even numbers, but the static prevented them from mating with each other. And so they spread and merged with the inanimate dust and wandered wherever fate decreed, almost indistinguishable from their environment.

Time passed. Quintessentially decimated, the spores continued, settling on cliff and plain, on animate and vegetative, rising into the sky and sinking into the water. Fungi fed upon them, and grazing herbivores. Some died and rotted, while others achieved the pinnacle and were destroyed by the fierce radiation of the upper sunlight. Some were buried, encysted, and lay dormant interminably, waiting for the destiny that did not come. Quintillions remained, distributed across the planet. Then quadrillions and finally only trillions.

Other spores from other ancients mixed with these: plants, molds, animates in countless species. The old one's spawn was long lost in the proliferation. Now there was no way to estimate their diminishing number, and seldom did any approach a sibling close enough to react to the repulsion. But some few did encounter similar spores released by other members of the species, and where sexually compatible they merged. Union had been completed, and the two spores became a single embryo.

Perhaps no more than a million of the old one's seed achieved such matings in the course of the fertile years, and for almost all it meant destruction. Merged, they had to grow—and there, was little opportunity for it. Where they landed they sprouted hyphae and formed cords of mycelium, seeking nourishment—but there was seldom anything they could use, since their diet was precise. Some seemingly similar embryos flourished in organic dust, and thousands competed for it vigorously, but the old one's minions perished there. Others fell upon carrion and reveled in the inert meat—but not these.

Time ran out. The mated spores grew without intake and bled their energies into extinction. Some were preyed upon by omnivorous animalcules. Some found suitable lodging, but could not grow, inhibited by inherent defects or harmful radiation or rough treatment or environmental incompatibility. Some grew too slowly, and were eliminated by rivals for the food, and some were unsuccessful mutants.

One endured all hazards and became established: a parasite upon the body of a tremendous beast. This one developed the characteristic symbol that would identify it as an individual for the rest of its lifetime: an intricate network representing a compromise between the symbols of its unknown parents. Cruder intellects would fashion it a geometric diamond with unimportant structural deviations.

Diam had achieved incipient sentience.

The host-beast charged and fought, and the unfelt parasites upon its skin were crushed and bruised and brushed away. Only Diam survived long enough, and at such time as to develop mobility before the host terminated its own violent existence in battle with another of its kind.

Diam tore free and fled, a leaping midget the size of an insect, before the body of the omnivore dissolved beneath the digestive secretions of its conqueror. Hitherto only chance had dictated his survival; now he had control, and would live or die depending upon his fitness. He lived. He preyed upon the baby omnivores feeding on dust and corpses, and he grew.

In time he encountered an adult of his kind: a full-grown carnivore. The manta took Diam in charge and helped him find proper sustenance. Others were similarly salvaged, until there was a flock of diversely parented hoppers: Diam and Circe and Star and Pent and Hex and Lin and sibling symbols. Secure, for a time, they grew fat and clumsy as they learned to communicate with each other and to recognize individual patterns.

Increasing size brought problems, for the aerodynamics of a creature weighing less than an ounce changed when it came to weigh more than a pound in a comparatively short segment of its life. Gravity became a significant and objectionable factor; a clumsy landing hurt. The tremendous growth rate kept Diam and his foster siblings continually off-balance, and the magnifying complexities of communication also strained their as yet diminutive faculties. So much was demanded!

Then, just as they were coming in sight of

mastery, they were given onerous instructions, taken to the place of decease, and there put into the charge of a blind alien omnivore. It was the beginning of an exile that they knew meant a lifelong separation from their kind for most of them, and dishonorable death.

The two-footed pseudo-omnivore stood over Pent's crushed body, its slick round-pebble orbs shifting whitely. The five-faceted symbol would speak no more; eye and brain had been crushed beneath the savage and abruptly knowledgeable force of the stranger.

It was good: the omnivore had proven itself. It had risen above the terrible limitations of its physique to meet a civilized creature on even terms. Now at last it was permissible to converse with it without restraint, while Pent dissolved into smoky spore vapors. The other omnivores had been innocuous pets, unable ever to comprehend the code of the warrior, unworthy to share the information of the elite. This one—this one was contemporary.

Diam took his stance before the clumsy artificial eye the omnivore had brought. It was uncomfortable, communicating via such a mechanism, but no more so than the concept of a sapient omnivore, or a world in which green plants retained their life to anchor on the ground and magnify grotesquely. If the stranger learned quickly, the machinery might soon be dispensed with.

The ball-eyed one gestured crudely with its forelimb. A pictorial representation took shape, so abbreviated that it was hard to follow. Surely there was some better way to do the job! Complete understanding would be extremely tedious if all communication had to be filtered through this obstruction.

The omnivore seemed to realize this. It sucked in more of the primitive fumes emerging from the burning container and returned to try again.

Then it began to learn. Ratios clarified, symbols danced through permutations, and the creature became more and more responsive to suggestion. A truly powerful intellect was beginning to emerge. But—an increasingly ill one.

"Like the slime mold!" it projected, showing in summary the life history of the local example. A slimy, jellylike plasmodium crept under the moist vegetable leaves fallen on the floor of the monster-plant forest, surrounding the organic matter it discovered and digesting it comfortably. Then, emerging into the light, the yellow creature shifted into inanimate status and fruited: brownish balls ascended slim orange stems and opened to release the floating spores; these, falling on water, germinated and put out tiny flagella to enable them to swim. Two came together and mated, found land and grew into the original slime formation.

"You actually evolved from the third kingdom— from fungi!" the omnivore stated, as though this were not obvious and reasonable. The parallel to the primitive slime mold was imperfect, but certainly such a creature could have been ancestral to all the sentients of Nacre. The astonishing thing was that it had not happened similarly on Earth. Here the fungal forms had failed to advance properly, while the plants overran the planet, and the animals—who neither created food from light and mineral nor broke down residues to complete the cycle— somehow had become dominant over it all. The notion of a life-form that served no useful purpose appearing and achieving sapience was appalling—but nevertheless a fact that had to be recognized.

These things maintained two discrete sexes throughout life, and generated their spores long before death. They omitted the atmospheric-floating stage entirely, preferring to confine their embryos within their living flesh.

What other monstrosities were to be found in the universe?

Circe, symbol of the circle, was to claim this episode, though Diam read it first:

"The mantas saw *us* as pets?" Aquilon demanded, amazed. "After we raised them and brought them all the way to Earth?"

"Not exactly. But it was hard for them to refrain from killing you as a matter of habit or instinct, without some innocuous designation." Subble watched her move about the apartment, her body lovely under the translucent shift. "They saw all three of you as omnivores from the start. They were soon aware of your diets—I mean, the mantas on Nacre were aware—not from any mysterious aura, but from simple observation. Veg had no flesh adhering to his teeth, and his breath reflected this, for example. They could see the microscopic particles in the air that we discern as smell. But the species Homo sapiens *is* omnivorous, and the attempted deviation of individual members is an oddity, apart from the oddity of the entire form of life. They could not imagine a *Nacre* omnivore settling down to graze peacefully among the herbivores. They marveled at this for a long time, wondering whether the inconsistency was a characteristic of the kingdom."

She came and sat in his lap and ran her hand over his cheek. "Then why did that one manta stop Veg and me from getting together? If it *knew* we were all of the same kind—"

Subble found the trigger-thread and pulled. Her shift fell open. "Because it did not fully understand the rules of your game. Your nature was omnivorous, but your practice deviated, not just dietetically but in your evident concern for each other. True omnivores never cooperate. It wanted to study the three of you, and for all it knew, Veg might be along solely to serve your hunger when the time came. Apart from its natural aversion to cannibalism—another omnivore trait—it wanted to fathom you as a group, and had to play safe until it was sure."

"Before we make love," she murmured, "there is something you should know."

"I know you are beautiful," he said.

She smiled—and with that expression her lovely features became flaccid, grotesquely homely. The vibrant body seemed to cave in on itself, becoming a mushy mannequin; the shape was there, but not the glory. It was the death of rapture.

Subble shoved her away. "That ties it. You were cured of that. I saw you smile, before."

He stood up and marched toward the lamp he now spotted on the floor. "I'm still under the hallucinogen. Damn overdose!" He reached to snuff it out, though it flared violently.

Circe erased the rest.

The mangled bodies had long since been eaten, the alien structures that were bones scattered, but the old stockade still seemed to reflect the night of ravage that had wiped out the off-world colony. Fungus grew richly out of the crevices of the tumbled buildings; dust and debris covered the inert machinery. Measured plots of Earth plants remained only in outline; they rotted where they had died when the mechanics who ran the sunlamps vanished.

Star moved on. Never before had his people slaughtered an entire population, and even traversing the scene in the eidetic memory provided by the elder who had been there was objectionable to him. He did not regret the action, for anything the group decided upon was proper, but he disliked the waste. These had been dangerous omnivores, yes, that insisted upon killing indiscriminately as was their nature, and so had set the precedent—but their flesh had proved to be of an entirely different order of construction and quite difficult to digest. Disposal of all eighteen bodies had been a terrible struggle—but the manta was bound to eat all it killed.

The aliens had seemed monstrous, with their inability to communicate, but subsequent developments had thrown into question their need to be put entirely out of their misery. Perhaps it would have been better to study them more carefully.

Then another party had descended from the blazing sky, and set up a more powerful base, preventing contact until a trio became isolated. The opportunity had come—if the individuals could be protected from the dangers of the world and their own quixotic nature. The first to spot them had lost them again as they fled in their machine; the second had died as they misunderstood his purpose. The third had made contact at night, and shepherded them to the place of dying, where the group could assemble. They were partly tame by then.

Then the ugliest omnivore had become less frightening. Star had it all in the transferred images, and it helped them comprehend the astonishing and descending mind of the present omnivore. These creatures were not entirely savage.

Diam:

"Report!"

Subble stood before the pickup of the Director's dais and spoke to the man or men who controlled him—men he had never seen. "I interviewed the three names on the list and determined that the problem involved them only indirectly. Each person provided a segment of their joint experience on the planet Nacre, but the whole remained incomplete. The key actually lay with the representatives of the dominant species of the planet, imported by the trio as theoretic pets and approved by quarantine as sterile and distributed among the three at the ratio of one, one and six when they resettled on Earth. The humans feared for the eventual security of these alien carnivores, so hid them diversely; and there were personal problems encouraging a temporary separation. These circumstances—"

"We are aware of the circumstances. Proceed."

Subble did not show surprise at this evidence of a

parallel investigation. "Full contact was not feasible until one of our own species earned the respect of the manta by meeting it in honorable battle. With them, as with us, physical appreciation must precede intellectual appreciation. I met their representative on an isolated beach and—"

"We know the details. Proceed."

This time he hesitated visibly. "It was an impasse. I finally took the hallucinogenic drug again in order to establish a close enough rapport with my opponent so that—"

"Naturally! Proceed."

"After I killed it, I realized that their fungoid nature was an appalling danger to—"

"Proceed!"

"Because Earth itself is now largely dependent upon—"

"Proceed!"

"The moment one dies—"

"Proceed!"

Subble leaped upon the dais and knocked aside the screen. A single manta stood there, glaring into the translating mechanism.

Subble grabbed the lamp and flung it against the wall. The oils poured out; the green flame expanded hungrily.

Diam faded from view. So did the dais and the rest of the set. There was only the heaving, animate fire.

"Next verse!" Subble cried.

Five mantas:

Subble stood on the sand watching Pent move. He had taken the drug before he killed the manta—

which meant that everything since the moment of inhalation was suspect, even the killing itself. He could trust none of it—and he could not risk igniting the lamp again.

Pent circled but did not charge. Why hadn't the creature killed him while he stood bemused by wish-fulfillments? What held it back now?

Was it afraid of mycotic hallucinogen? Did the drug that induced spurious images in the mind of a man have a similar effect on the manta? Or was the result more severe, for it?

His hand hovered over the lamp, hesitating to snuff it out.

Then he realized: he had tried to kill that flame twice—and had not succeeded. He had merely stepped into a new sequence. What guarantee did he have that this was not yet another nightmare, and the lamp an illusion?

How could he put it out—if the act of quenching it was itself a dream?

Subble smiled. The manta hadn't attacked because it did not understand his ploy. Why should he stand on land, after establishing that his tactical posture was deficient there? Why—unless he had come up with something special?

And perhaps he had. He was not the same man who had begun the contest. The things he saw were entirely different now. He appreciated Pent in a new and marvelous perspective, and would not react as he had before. The information had been delivered hallucinogenically, as though he had been listening to the manta's quarter of the story, immersing himself in it as he had during the human quarters— but that did not mean that it was invalid.

On the contrary. He must have killed Pent and earned contact, learning to interpret the peripheral signals, to operate without dependency upon the transceiver. The drug made his mind responsive to suggestion, even alien suggestion. When he had taken it in the presence of the manta he had recreated the world-view of the manta, and had seen to some extent what the manta saw, modified somewhat by his humanity. Somewhat. . . .

Yet Pent circled still, alive. He could as easily have invented the entire thing, including the fungal origins of the manta. Was he victor or vanquished?

Twice the vision had become dominated by his own ambitions—and twice he had realized this and cut it off. Agents were not supposed to be subject to ambition. Such visions indicated personality break-down, making him unsuitable a\ an agent. He had been moved by beautiful Aquilon's body, so he had recreated her in a willing situation, much as he might have done subconsciously had he possessed a differentiated subconscious. Balked, he had jumped ahead, then, to the completion of his mission—and perceived the distortion more readily, that time.

The drug affected his perception, making real any transitory thought that had sufficient force. He had taken an overdose, but it did not impair his reasoning facilities—*faculties!*—or his memory. He had entered a world of hallucinations—but he could control them.

At this moment he was matching hal—*ill*usion to reality. He could now snuff out the flame successfully—and did not need to. Assuming that his reasoning were valid. Otherwise he was trapped anyway.

He tested. The genie Myco appeared, grinning. "Put on your turban!" Subble said. The slave obeyed.

"Kill Pent."

"Master, Pent is dead already." The language was wrong; Myco should not be speaking modern.

"Well, kill him again!"

"Gladly!" Myco volumned up, launched enormous jeweled hands at Subble's throat.

The five watched him die, unable to protect the omnivore from himself. Contact had been a failure after all.

Cal woke with a start, the dream fading. Strange, the way it had become an obsession: the simple fact of drinking the blood of the Nacre omnivore. He knew now that he had suffered from the same compulsion syndrome that Veg and Aquilon had— except that they had not possessed the intellectual determination to carry it to such a macabre extreme. The simple refusal to eat meat, or to smile—but *he* had made of his entire life a nightmare, like the man who believed he must commit a crime every day or die. Cal had taken unto himself the action he considered most reprehensible: the parasitic consumption of the blood of other animals.

Though the origin was psychasthenic, the effects were real. He had wanted to die, and for years had driven himself to it, fighting the internal censors of self-preservation . . . only to be balked at the climax by the blind faith of friends. A man who gave of his strength, a woman who bled herself—to show their faith in *him*.

He opened his eyes and saw Star standing at the window. Was someone coming?"

That had been the breaking point, he thought, resuming the chain. They had beaten him, for he could not bring himself to sacrifice either the man or the woman he loved to his own morbidity. Veg would have driven himself, like a faithful horse, to a running collapse, traveling two miles loaded for every mile while the others went unburdened. Aquilon would have bled herself dry—to save the feeble creature they called friend. The two had overcome his death-wish by tripling the cost of success. Better that he should live, than they die.

And so he had been given the impetus for change, and had searched for a pretext. He had taken the blood of the omnivore and thrived upon it— knowing, beneath a new suppression, that it was a nutrient fluid unrelated to human or Earthly blood except in general function. How could it be blood— drawn from the corpse of an animate fungus? And from that first exhilarating step, that concession to the needs of life and health, he had progressed steadily toward a more normal diet, and gained back much of the strength the years had dissipated.

Yet, like Aquilon, he had replaced his chains with stronger ones. He had accepted life for himself—at the possible expense of that of his species. Thus his new nightmare stemmed from that cup of blood— Aquilon's or Nacre's, he was not sure—and climaxed in rivers of the blood of man drenching the earth of Earth.

"Wake and dress immediately," the voice said, and for a moment it seemed the manta had spoken. "I will carry you."

That was what had disturbed Star. A man *had* been approaching. "Subble!" he said. "Did you—?"

"No. I am Sueve, assigned to complete this aspect of the mission. Subble is otherwise occupied."

Cal dressed hurriedly. Now he heard the movements of trucks outside, of human activity. "What's going on?"

"Evacuation." Sueve picked him up and strode to the door.

"But my books, my notes—"

"Sorry. Nothing but yourself. Your clothing will be destroyed when you enter decontamination."

"What's *happening?*" But Sueve did not reply. He was running now, down the street that covered the length of the beach establishments, avoiding the slowly maneuvering army trucks and confused, milling people, while Star kept up easily. The wind whistled by Cal's ear; the agent was astonishingly strong and swift.

It was early dawn, still too dark for the birds to sing. The greens and whites and browns of the plaster and wood houses were only shades of gray. "Truth is a shade of gray," he thought, and wondered who had said it first. Now and then the gulf was visible, its water dark and still. Palmettoes and pines leaned over the winding street, and large century plants spoked beside it. The bright signs of the all-night stores, the motels and restaurants catering to restless tourists, these shone eerily in the absence of their proprietors and clientele. The evacuation was almost complete already, proceeding with a swiftness he had not thought possible as the sealed trucks moved out. The drivers wore bacterial masks. But there were no sirens, no shrill radio exhortations or loudspeaker warnings. All was accomplished silently. Why?

Sueve was cutting across the barbered golf links. In the center of the convoluted greens stood a ship. A booster rocket, grossly misplaced here. Then they were inside. Sueve—so much like Subble!—set the controls and tied Cal into a deep acceleration couch, while Star braced against what was coming.

"What happens to all the other people? Why them, too?"

"They are being interned for the duration." The panel was clicking off the countdown.

Yet he was sure there had been no declaration of war, no reports of oncoming hurricane or other natural calamity. This was a sudden, complete and secret evacuation of the beaches—and he could think of only one reason. The one he had dreamed about so guiltily.

"What about the ones who refuse to go? Who demand reasons? Who hide, who are missed?"

"They remain." The rocket ignited and acceleration crushed him back into sleep.

The line of men in fire suits combed through the forest, driving everything before them by spraying a toxic chemical. Where they passed, the green foliage wilted and dead insects and small animals littered the leafy floor.

"Hey!" Hank Jones exclaimed. "This is *my* land! Get outta here!"

Then, seeing that they paid him no attention, he took up his axe. "Go get Veg!" he yelled to Job. "He'll help. Tell 'im it's an invasion—they're laying down mustard gas!"

Job bolted as the second line of invaders, masked and armed, conducted Hank away. Job leaped over the wall and pounded down the trail to the neighboring work area.

But Veg was the major object of the advance. He had problems of his own, that early morning, as the troops converged.

Hex, knowing the meaning of the weapons and the spray and the hovering ring of helicopters, permitted himself to be herded in with Veg. The omnivore had little sense of individual ethics. The only defense here was no defense.

Behind them, as the flyer lifted, the reluctant smoke of burning greenwood pushed up from the dying forest.

Joe looked up from his computer flow chart, but there was nothing in the hall. The noise came from the air circulation vents: not a hiss, not the usual knocking of incipient breakdown, but a subtle change in rhythm, as though the texture of the air had changed. A fine haze emerged.

He reached for his phone. He had authorized no addition of chemicals, and certainly not so unselectively as via the air. What was good for the rabbits was not necessarily good for the hens, and—

He slumped over his chart, letting the receiver fall. In their cages the animals also slumped. In minutes all were dead.

Incendiary gas now descended from the vents, filling the chambers. A spark, and it burned fiercely but not explosively, charring everything in almost complete silence. The farm had become a thorough oven by the time someone realized that there had been a small error: the man was supposed to have been evacuated first.

Circe alone escaped. She well knew the nature of the omnivore, and had been alert for the telltale sónic waves of the first faint preparations. She sped for the elevator before closure was complete. Its mechanism was powered by the same trunk line as the air circulators, and by the time the omnivores realized their oversight, Circe was out of the death zone.

But Aquilon's apartment too was a trap. Woman and manta were caught and sealed in a pressurized capsule: air and water but not freedom. The capsule was taken from the building secretly as the suited demolition crew razed the apartment, burning the furnishings and paintings and melting down all other fixtures.

The faceless units of the incendiary crews moved relentlessly, guiding their tanks delicately down the length of the beaches spraying gasoline and igniting it with bursts from the flame throwers. Men ran screaming from the fired houses: the ones who had avoided relocation by intent or mistake, fearing the quarantine stations, the loss of their expensive properties and household possessions, or just plain ornery about their rights. The omnivore cared nothing for their rights. They ran, touched by jets from the tanks, their clothing and then their skin dropping from their bodies in bright embers, and after them their women and children, crying skinlessly. Some tried to attack the massive tanks that crushed their homes—and were themselves crushed beneath the unswerving metal treads. Some dived into the ocean, swimming beneath the hovering white-breasted gulls, and the burning oils pursued them across the water, converting the gray-green depths to orange and black.

It was swift, it was merciless. Lin, symbol of the line, paced the length of it, observing the omnivore in action. What the tanks did not destroy, the napalm bombers did. By the time the sun appeared in the sky, the beaches for a hundred miles had been leveled. If anything survived there, it regretted it.

Lin left, urged by time and the increasing light. Beyond the beaches the nets extended, reaching far into the sea and penning all surface marine creatures behind them. Ships patrolled this perimeter—robot vessels, armored, no man upon them, diffusing deadly fluids to plumb the lowest regions. Automatic weapons shot down everything that approached from either side—flights of birds, a straying pilot, even large insects. Here, too, the closure was complete.

Lin joined the others at the robot shuttle that bore them rapidly away, but he knew what happened behind. A single missile arched over land and water, homing in on an isolated island. A hundred feet above the tiny beach where Subble lay it disappeared.

The island became a ball of incandescence as land and water vaporized.

Where it had been, a monstrous mushroom sprouted.

"You mean—*everything's* gone?" Aquilon asked, shocked. "Veg's forest, the whole cellar farm, all the gulf beaches?"

"They had to go," Cal said. They were crowded

with the seven mantas into an orbiting chamber awaiting decontamination: a thoroughly unpleasant process. "There is no other way to be *sure*—and even the two hours they allowed for evacuation before . . . liquidation were a calculated risk."

"I don't get it," Veg said. "Why did they leave us alone so long—no quarantine, no trouble—then suddenly, pow!"

"Because it took the bureaucracy some time to become aware of the danger. They suspected that the mantas might revert to a dangerous wild state, or something minor like that, I think. When Subble figured it out and made his report, they had to act immediately. We're extremely fortunate they decided to save our lives; that surprises me, as a matter of fact."

"*What* danger? The mantas have no diseases, and they know they aren't supposed to attack people."

Cal sighed. "It is complicated, but I'll try. Briefly, the danger is inherent in the nature of the mantas and the other creatures of Nacre. They are of a fungus world, where animals of our type never evolved at all. The mantas are the most advanced representatives of the third kingdom. They are in fact evolved from parasitic fungi resembling our slime molds, while the ones we call herbivores are similarly advanced saprophytes. Naturally they couldn't be true herbivores, with no living vegetation on the planet's surface, and they certainly aren't plants themselves."

"I never thought of that!" Veg exclaimed. "No trees, no grass, no flowers—"

"Then—they aren't really animals, even?" Aquilon wanted to know.

"Not as we think of them. Parallel evolution has brought the Nacre animates to a state surprisingly similar to the higher Earth animals, which is why we made the mistake we did. But their life cycle remains mycotic—that is, they reproduce by spores, and at some period they are unable to move independently."

"But so do Earth fungi," Aquilon said.

"Precisely. And Earth fungi are exceedingly important to Earth's economy, as I explained to Subble. So important that no interference with their development and exploitation can be tolerated. If we lost our food-yeasts alone, billions of people would starve before alternatives were developed. And if the carbon-dioxide cycle were broken—"

Veg was shaking his head dubiously, and Aquilon seemed uncertain also. He kept forgetting that although they had been on Nacre, the chemistries of ecology meant little to them. But there were other facets.

"Can you imagine what havoc would be wreaked in our civilization if an octillion super-advanced fungus spores were released in our atmosphere to mix with those here? There could be millions of mantas overrunning the planet, looking for omnivores —*men,* that is—to feed upon; and the next generation would see more mantas than men in the world."

They looked at him, trying to visualize it.

"Or the spores might succeed in merging with local spores to produce Earth-Nacre half-breeds that might very well displace all other life on Earth. The mantas by themselves, you see, are self-limiting; they feed only on omnivores, whether animal or fungus, and have the intelligence and conscience to preserve some equitable balance. Man can live with them, though perhaps not as master. But the half-breeds could be—"

"Omnivores," Aquilon breathed. "Beasts with *no* controls. . . ."

"Worse. They could operate on the molecular level, and start our common molds and yeasts changing, leapfrogging freakishly along the path of a billion years of evolution. That's what would hit our food supply. We are able to work so effectively with our fungi because they are primitive. But we know now that their evolution can lead to forms in many ways superior to us. Since most mutations are not beneficial, all life as we understand it today could be imperiled while savage semi-primitive strains competed for dominance. Our yeasts could begin feeding on *us*."

"But I thought different species could not mate unless they were closely related," Aquilon said. "The Nacre spores should be quite different from ours."

"Perhaps. Perhaps not. We know so little about the third kingdom that we just can't be certain. There is no such thing as complete convergence in the animal kingdom—but spores are about as hardy and versatile an instrument of reproduction as exists. Some may grow to maturity without mating, but ingest other spores they encounter. Alien enzymes in a local predator could result in modification. There are so many billions of spores in our atmosphere that some kind of mutation becomes a probability rather than a possibility. The danger is theoretical— but so great that every vestige of alien life must be expunged from the planet. Our existence may depend upon it."

Veg thought about it, obviously following only

part of the technical discussion. "We've been back on Earth several months and I haven't seen any new things appearing. Why all the hurry now? All the—burning."

"And why *did* they capture us and the mantas alive?" Aquilon added.

"I think they did it because they had to get the mantas alive, or completely sealed in at death, and that would have been almost impossible without us. We're the only ones who actually associate with mantas; they'll come with us, while they might never be captured alive in a hunt."

"Yeah, but—"

"You see, the creatures of Nacre don't spore until death. In the natural course, as I make it, they dissolve into spores at the end of an active life. But if they anticipate death, they can prime themselves for emergency reproduction. They're sexless in the active stage, actually; the spores are the ones that mate. So an individual manta can release a complete collection of spores, and ours are primed for it, even though they are not full grown. If any die now, their bodies will quickly fall apart into billions of spores—and the siege is on. Each is a hopping bomb, on Earth."

Aquilon looked at the mantas. "I see," she said soberly. "They don't *want* to die, but if they do, the species goes on."

"Yes. The only safe procedure is live capture and deportation—and sterilization of the territory they occupied, no matter what the cost. Any person, any animal, any gust of wind could carry devastating spores. Everything that leaves the zones of exposure has to be decontaminated, and those who refuse to leave—"

"What about *us?*"

"We're isolated now. I suppose we'll be exiled to Nacre. Perhaps they'll let us return once the mantas are landed there."

"To Earth?" Veg remarked sourly. "After they burned my lot? I'd rather stay on Nacre."

"I would, too," Aquilon agreed. "I didn't know how—close—Earth felt until I came back. I—" She looked at the mantas. "One of them is missing! What happened to it?"

"I'm afraid Subble killed it. That would have been what precipitated—this. They only burned the forest and cleaned out your room, but the mantas' island—"

They looked out the vision screen and watched the enormous cloud below. The station was orbiting at such a distance that they remained above the general area of the gulf, but even so the effect could be discerned.

"The spores were already in the air—" Aquilon murmured.

"Why would he do a thing like that?" Veg demanded. "He seemed like a pretty straight guy to me, considering."

"And me," Aquilon whispered.

"We may never know. He went to meet the six mantas on the island last night; that's all I know."

"And he didn't return . . ." she said, staring down.

Diam, reading the compressions and rarefactions of the ambient gases by which these omnivores communicated, understood, just as he had finally grasped the terminal signals of the stronger omnivore on the island. The Subble-creature had achieved

219

dominant status by meeting Pent honorably and crushing him, but even as full communication was attained he was reeling from severe distortion of perception. Subble's intellect, once unmasked, had been monstrously powerful; had the ritual conflict been mental instead of physical, he could have mastered them all in concert. They had had to change off to assimilate it all, even though his mind had wandered erratically and finally lost contact entirely as he died. They had drawn from him all the information they could, and tried to give him what he had come for, but by the time they understood the situation it was too late for him.

Their presence on Earth was already forfeit. Pent's spores would not produce new mantas; the conditions were wrong, and there were no matching spores from others of their kind. But the risk of mutation did exist.

They had come to comprehend, not to destroy. Destruction was a characteristic of the omnivore, not the manta. This was a wilderness world without true order; the life forms were far more vigorous and tenacious than those they had known. But Subble had approached sentience, and his kind deserved its chance.

The omnivore was savage, but with certain redemptions. Diam had known what would happen when he activated Subble's equipment and made the coded report Subble would have made, had his overdrugged mind not destroyed itself. Diam had modified the report only to protect his brothers and the three original contactees, seeing that desire in the man's mind at the end. The omnivore had done his

best, and it was proper that his victory and his
sacrifice be honored.

The three lesser omnivores—whose minds, Diam
now realized, were also far more powerful than his
own, but almost entirely nullified by their physical
and sensory limitations—these three had problems
he could not comprehend. But it was better to give
them the chance to work them out together, than to
leave them at the mercy of the corporate omnivore.
None of them would have survived that.

Yet his major thought was with Subble, who had
expired the way he wanted to: with his mission. Now
Subble's incandescence blended with that of the
periwinkles and sand dollars and fiddler crabs and
Pent's incipient spores, and it was fitting.

SCIENCE FICTION AND FANTASY
FROM AVON ◆ BOOKS

INTIMACY . . .
BEYOND ECSTASY . . .
BEYOND TIME . . .

MINDBRIDGE

BY NEBULA AND HUGO AWARD WINNER

JOE HALDEMAN

"FANTASTIC . . . A MINDBLITZ
. . . BRINGS OUT ALL THE TERROR WE REPRESS AT
THE POSSIBILITY OF HOW EASILY WE MIGHT BE
POSSESSED BY A STRONGER POWER."
Los Angeles Times

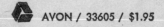 AVON / 33605 / $1.95

MIND 7-79